#80

and other dog stories

ALICE WOLLMAN

Published by Alice Wollman
Identifiers: LCCN 2018904997
ISBN (print) 978-1-7321397-0-1
ISBN (e-book) 978-1-7321397-1-8
Subjects: 1. Dogs-Fiction 2. Human-Animal Relationships-Fiction 3. Biography 4.
Brittany Dogs

Cover Design: Lieu Pham, Covertopia.com
Cover Image: Alice Wollman
Cover Model: Leona Valley's Sonny Red Side Up "Red"
Publisher: Alice Wollman with Amazon Publishing
Editor: Janet Fullwood.
Except, "The Field Trial", edited by Joe Gower
Book layout: Guido Henkel

For Grizzly

"If there are no dogs in Heaven, then when I die I want to go where they went."

—Will Rogers

Foreword

Numbers. They can be significant, especially when we're talking about lottery numbers, driver's licenses, birthdays or personal bests. They can be quite insignificant, as when we are speaking of numbers of candies in a jar or the number of times you've said something, forgotten something or, in this case, when you are speaking of a sad little orange and white dog. Don't get me wrong. This dog is not insignificant in any way. She's far from that. However, there was a time when she was unknown. She was just one in a large group of orange and white dogs trying to survive and trying to be significant.

In this life-changing, thought-provoking, heartwarming book, you'll follow her journey from being defined as "Number Eighty" to becoming the much-loved, quirky, beautiful Miss Hedlee that she is today: triumphant over tragedy. Along the way, you'll meet Hedlee's adopted brothers and sisters, her human mom and dad and her aunties and uncles. You will laugh and you will cry. You will get angry and you will question. Most of all, you will get an honest and heartfelt glimpse into the life of a rescued dog who is adopted into a loving home that contains an eclectic cast of characters. You'll meet Grizzly, the handsome jock; Fred, his goofy brother; Buddy, the keeper; Annie, the golden girl; and Annie's puppies, who each come with their own budding personalities.

Some of these stories will be told by the dogs themselves, and some in the voice of Alice. While there is humor and insight into life with Brittany dogs, there is also truth and honesty, which are often lacking. As most dog parents know, dogs will provide you with some of the happiest days in your life. They will also provide you with some of the saddest.

Alice and I have laughed, cried, discussed many a bodily function and anguished together over decisions and choices that we, as dog moms, have had to make. I can think of no one who is more deserving of the success that comes with stories well told. With that said, turn off the television, grab a box of tissues, snuggle with your four-leggeds and settle in for a heck of a read.

Janice Gantenbein
Dog Trainer
DAJAZOO

Preface

Can a book be written by accident? Since I just finished writing a book that I didn't intend to write, I guess it is possible. I like to write essays for friends and family. I have done so for many years. Nearly all the essays in this book were meant to stand alone, meaning each could be published individually, which is why some background information about a dog or circumstance might be repeated. Since dogs can't talk, I often interpreted what each dog was trying to tell me, and I hope I got it right. If there are typographical or grammatical errors, I will do exactly what you might do at your own home. I will sheepishly blame these faux pas on the dog.

I can tell you, I have spilled a lot of tears and have had plenty of laughs writing these vignettes. My only hope is that I did my Brittanys justice by telling their stories, for each dog has been a blessing in my life. I can only hope their tales are a blessing in yours, too.

Alice Wollman (2018)

ONE

#80: JULY 2013

Torrential rains pelted all morning as we diligently worked on getting the dogs ready for transport. It was an unusually cold, dark and gloomy summer day for Louisiana. We slowly but steadily loaded the big transport truck with the last of the Magnolia dogs. It was an awful day, but somehow, we got through it. We placed the last dog inside the vehicle and said goodbye to the huge semi-truck. Just as we were pulling out of the parking lot, the rain stopped, the sun came out and there was an enormous rainbow over the top of the Raceland Agricultural Facility. At that moment, I knew everything was going to be OK. Thinking about it now still makes me cry. It was as if God parted the clouds with his beautiful rainbow and said, "Thank you."

Sue Janowski
Rescue Volunteer
Operation Magnolia Brittany Rescue

TWO
#80: DAY 1

I am nothing. I am on a long chain with others who look like me. The thick air weighs heavily upon my chest. Mosquitos bite my ears and I scratch. I smell sickness on the line. The others are not as strong. Their breath is heavy as death whispers in their ears. Something is thrown at us. We eat it quickly before the ants come and take their quarry. I want to stretch, but I cannot move more than two feet in any direction. I try to pull the chain wrapped around my neck, but it hurts. I need to pee. I let it go and it quickly spreads upon the earth. I sit in my own urine. I have no choice. I want to yell, but I can't. I am nothing.

THREE

#80: DAY 2

I am nothing. I suck in the thick, wet air as if it is nourishment because I am hungry. I hear noises. Rumbling. Doors slamming. Men and women in uniforms. Others are unloading metal boxes. Lots of boxes. Someone kneels next to me and yells, "Get me the bolt cutters, this one is hurt!" The chain is imbedded in my skin and I cry. I shake. I don't mean to, but I pee. They release me from the chain and liquid oozes onto my fur. A lady gently rubs my head and puts stuff on my neck. They place me in a box. I am loaded onto a truck. Someone writes something and assigns it to me. I am no longer "nothing".

I am #80.

FOUR
#80: DAY 3

My name is #80. I am part of something called a triage. That means they separate us by need and sickness. They test for parasites that are living in the arteries, lungs and hearts of my family. I can smell the worm, but humans need to test for it. The infestation is spread by infected mosquitos. The larvae eat through the skin and connective tissue before reaching the blood stream. Once in the blood, the worms are transported to the arteries and lungs, which will cause blood clots or congestive heart failure. Most of my family will test positive. I am one of the few that is negative, and I don't know if being negative is bad or good. They write on my tag a new, bigger name: #80 Hedlee H-N

They give me a bath, which is frightening but comforting at the same time. A lady puts water on me and rubs my back and it feels wonderful. She tells me I am a good girl.

I watch as the Man pushes something pointy into the skin of some of my family and they fall asleep forever. It takes a long time for them to fall asleep because they are sick. Seven sleep and don't wake up. I am sad. Then the Man comes to me with a pointy thing and he uses it on my neck and rubs my head. They say it is to protect me. It hurts a little bit, but I don't fall asleep forever. I am lucky. They keep me here until they decide what to do. There are ninety-six of us left. In a couple of weeks, four more will die. The rest of us wait, and we hope.

The best part of today is that I have my own box. My food is not thrown onto the ground. I have my own bowl and I don't have to worry about someone taking my food. That part makes me happy, but I am very scared. At least I am not asleep forever. I now have a name. That means I have an identity. I am not nothing; nor am I just #80. I am #80 Hedlee H-N.

FIVE

#80: DAY 4

My name is #80 Hedlee H-N. I have been transported to a place where we are sorted and separated. The doctor put me to sleep for a little while. I wake up with an ouch. I am groggy and I go back to sleep. When I wake up again, there is food just for me. I don't have to share. There are lots of people who take care of us and tell us we are good. Our fur is groomed and shaved short. They treat us for bug bites and ouches and give us play time. We continue to wait to find out our fate. Of the 103 dogs rescued, seven are now asleep. Before they took a nap forever, each dog was given a name and a kiss goodbye. For some reason, it is important for them to get a name. A name means they mattered. I guess I matter too, because they gave me a name. My name is #80 Hedlee H-N.

SIX
#80: DAY 30, AFTERNOON

My name is #80 Hedlee H-N. I am in a place where there are lots of others that bark, bark, bark. We are separated by wire links. We stand on concrete. There are sixteen that look like me. We are Brittany dogs. I have been here a long time. Each day, a few more disappear. I think no one wants me. I wait for a foster to come but the others leave and I wait. I am scared. I won't come out of my kennel. I don't want anyone to see me, so I hide in the box. Then I hear words about me, "Hedlee's foster is here."

That's me! They bring me out with a rope on my neck. They drag me. I am afraid to come out. A lady kneels beside me. Oh, my gosh! She is going to touch my head! I shrink down low to the ground but it happens anyway. She hooks me to a leash and hands the rope back to the guard. The lady picks me up and puts me in a wire box in her car. She talks in a squeaky voice and she smells like flowers. She gives me a cookie and tells me I am a good girl. Her eyes are leaking but she is happy. She says, "Happy tears, Hedlee." She starts the car. Our new journey begins.

The drive is long. She talks to me and tells me about my new home. There are three others like me and one that looks different. I am getting a Foster Dad who will teach me about being a field dog. My Foster Mom is going to take me to school to learn how to sit and stay. I shake and I listen. The new Mom describes where I am going to live. It is a ranch. There are moo-moos and nay-nays all around. The town has hills and valleys. Beyond the hills is a desert. When I gain confidence, I will run with my new brothers in the desert. I don't know what a run is, but I want it. She says we are going to live in a house. I have never lived inside. I don't know what this means. She stops talking and she sings to me using my new name. "They call her Hedlee, Hedlee, faster than lightning. No one you see, is smarter than she." Now I know my real name. ♥ Hedlee

SEVEN

#80: DAY 30, EVENING

My name is Hedlee. We drive on a tree-lined street with split-rail fencing and rolling terrain. Foster Mom pushes a button and noise surrounds me. She tells me, "That is music Hedlee, Mozart's Symphony Number 40." I don't know what that is, but I close my eyes and it makes me feel protected and calm. We turn left, right and then left again; the car drives on dirt. When we stop, the music stops, too. My new Mom opens my box and puts me on the ground. She tries to walk me on a leash, but I jump all around, scared. I try to run away, but I can't, because I am attached to the leash. She gives me encouragement and walks me around the property, making one big loop so I can smell everything. After we awkwardly walk in a giant circle, Foster Mom takes me to these things that rise from the ground and go to an opening. She walks on the things but I don't know how. She walks back down, picks me up, and carries me through the opening.

When we go through the square, it is like another world. There is a man in there who is really big. His skin is ruddy and he has light fur on his head and some on his mouth. He says my name, "Hedlee!" I wag my tail, but it stays low between my legs. They take me to the other side of the room and we all go back outside together but in a different direction. My foster parents sit on something called a deck while I investigate an enclosed smaller yard. I pee and kick and I feel happy.

There is an ache in my heart and I don't know what it means. I investigate it. I slowly approach the new Mom. I climb closer and closer, stretching my neck really far. I touch my mouth to her face. Her eyes turn wet and she smiles. Then I do the same thing to the Man and his eyes turn wet, too, and he smiles. I sit between them and they rub my back.

The night is quiet and I am tired. Too tired to even eat. I climb on my new Mom's lap, rest my head on her shoulder and go to sleep. My slumber is absent of worry and fear. It is not just the feeling of being safe and comfortable. It is so much more. This is the first time in my entire life that I know I am truly loved. ♥ Hedlee

EIGHT

#80: DAY 32

My name is Hedlee. My Foster Mom took me to the vet. Dr. Dave did lots of poking and prodding. He was nice and said I was good. I was re-tested for the diseases that are common in Louisiana. Most importantly, my tests came back. I am NOT heartworm positive! Woo-hoo! BUT, I do have something bad in my body and must wait a few days before I can play with the dog boys. I get ear medicine in the morning and mouth medicine at night. I don't like the medicine but it will make me better.

There is good news! I discovered there is another dog in the house! Each time we go to the sleep room I find a dog waiting in there for me. She is very pretty and we touched our noses. My nose is soft, but this girl has a hard-cold nose. When I bark, she barks! When I wag my tail, she wags her tail! When I go into the room with the white bowl, she follows me but is really hard to find. I stand up on my hind legs and look above the counter where the people run water, and there she is! She smiles at ME!!! I like my new friend! ♥ Hedlee

NINE

#80: DAY 33

My name is Hedlee. The dog boys have been living outside until I get medical clearance. But I knew there was someone else living in the house besides me! I smell it. It lurks in the night and I hear it make noises in the closet. This morning it came out and growled at me! Me! The creature's tail turned big and it arched its back. I wanted to chase it but Foster Mom said "No!" I will sit and watch it. I desperately think it needs to be chased. It stares at me with contempt, slapping its tail all around and eating wet food that should belong to just me. I will steal the wet stuff when it is not looking. ♥ Hedlee

TEN

#80: DAY 35

My name is Hedlee. Last night I met the dog boys. It was overwhelming. They met me one at a time and not all together because that would have been too much! The first one was a BIG Brittany. He loved me very much. He wanted to play and was jumping around and wagging his tail like I was his new best friend. He was too wild for me and I got scared and hid behind the pillows on the couch. He didn't mind. He went and played in the front yard and then the next dog came to see me. He was even BIGGER and did not look like me. He didn't care if I was there or not. He was happy to be inside with his family. He drank some water; smelled me and walked away. I REALLY wanted to play with this boy, but he barked and said NO! He wanted to go outside with the BIG Brittany. Our Mom let him outside. The third dog came in and I LOVED him right away. He is small, like me. He didn't get in my face but he was interested in me. I wagged my tail and sat with him. Then we played. He is very gentle and I like that. Today, I am spending the day with the smallest Brittany. He is my new best friend. His name is Fred. ♥ Hedlee

ELEVEN

#80: DAY 36

My name is Hedlee Lamarr Benoit. A little over a month ago, no one could ever have guessed that a dog like me from rural Louisiana could end up in Hollywood, California. Today, I was within the shadow of the Hollywood sign. Well, all I could see was the "Ho" in the sign. The rest was blocked. But who would have guessed that I, Miss Hedlee, would be under the world famous "Ho" sign? Hollywood is full of very important people who like to be seen and known for their greatness.

Today my Foster Mom took me to work. She had to meet a client in one of the most affluent neighborhoods around. We drove on winding narrow roads with homes clustered tightly together on microscopic lots, hidden behind privacy gates so no one can see inside. We climbed up thoroughfares so thin, it was difficult for a single car to pass through. After a lot of twists and turns up Beachwood Drive, we took a sharp right turn onto a private lane and parked. Whew! Mom picked me up to put me on the smallest but only patch of grass available so I could pee. She was careful to carry me so that my paws would not touch the very hot asphalt pavement. Before she could place me on the green, I barfed all over her fancy business suit. Good thing she had a change of clothes and a dog-friendly client.

I am not Rin Tin Tin, Lassie, or even a Beverly Hills Chihuahua. Those Hollywood creations are not based on reality. I will never be perfect. I probably won't save Timmy from whatever mischief he may find, and I am certainly not small enough to fit in a designer handbag like a Beverly Hills dog. I am going to make mistakes. I will barf on my Mom, who now knows I get car sick. I am a three-year-old dog that to my own embarrassment and chagrin is getting potty trained like a puppy. And yes, it was I who left my golden nugget in the toy aisle for Mom to clean up at PetSmart. I am a beginner, and I am learning.

As a rescue dog, I have been through a lot, and now I have catching up to do. That is my reality. Do you know who the real heroes are in this world? Not the movie stars, the well-to-do people who hide behind a gated façade. It is the judge who ordered that I and my hundred-plus dog friends be seized; it is the people who came and got us and cared for us; it is the vet and assistants who checked us over and gave many of my siblings emergency treatment; and it is the unknown many who transferred us to foster homes all over the country so that, just a short month later, Miss Hedlee Lamarr of Louisiana, could sit beneath the shadow of the Hollywood sign with someone who loves and cares for a dog like me. To those unsung heroes from far and wide, I thank you. ♥ Hedlee

TWELVE

#80: DAY 40

My name is Hedlee. Sometimes we don't see the whole story by looking at a face, for often it is just a façade.

I had a great time playing with my new friend Fred. I can learn a lot from him because he has eight years' experience as the family dog. Today we dug a hole together, stole meow-meow food and ran around when it started to rain. I ran circles around Fred, literally. He thought that was funny. Then we took turns getting towel dried and brushed by Mom.

The big dogs came inside late in the day. The Britt named Grizzly really wanted to play with me again. He hopped around and wiggled his bottom in the air and jumped right near me. I screamed as if he bit me even though he did not. I ran away and hid. Mommy went and picked me up and made me feel better. Even Grizzly came to comfort me and approached me cautiously with a lick on my paw. He was sorry even though he did nothing wrong. Mommy studied my face and examined my scars. She knows what is wrong with me. Before I moved here, a big dog bit me on the nose and cheek. The scars are plain as day. The dog boys all understand. Take it slow with me, because I am afraid of dogs like me. ♥ Hedlee

THIRTEEN

#80: DAY 42

My name is Hedlee, and I am a thief. It was small stuff at first. Some cat food, a toy, someone's half eaten chewy bone. But then I started to grab bigger and better items. Last night I watched Foster Mom while she played with her I-Phone. She put it down to get Dad a drink. How was I supposed to know that the phone was attached to a cord? That is how I was caught. Darn, I could have had my own phone!

Today I went to retrieve even better things. I removed pillows from the couch and hid one in my crate. I didn't think they would notice, because there were a bunch more (Oh, they noticed!). The best find was when Mom was taking a shower: I stole her underwear, so she had none to wear when she toweled herself dry. Then I took her towel. That was funny!

The best thing I stole cannot be bought. I imagine if we could buy it, there would be a line all the way around the world for this special thing. For in the last week, I know I must have stolen a pawful of hearts and a lot of puppy kisses. You cannot buy real love anywhere. It is earned. ♥ Hedlee

FOURTEEN

#80: DAY 60

My name is Hedlee. The weird thing about living here is my Foster Mom's obsession with giving me a bath. I never had a bath when I lived in Louisiana. Now, I have a bath ONCE A WEEK! I never know when it is going to happen. One minute the family is sitting there watching television, and the next thing I know, I am carried away and deposited in the double porcelain kitchen sink. I have no say so in this fiasco? Of course not! It's only my body, my fur, my mud! The key word is "mine."

Tonight, it happened again. Foster Mom took off my collar. This is a special field-dog collar. It has my Foster Dad's name on a brass plate riveted to the leather. The brass plate has my foster home address, my Foster Dad's phone number and my Foster Mom's phone number. Just for back up, our neighbor, Dr. Dave put an itty-bitty chip under the skin in my neck. You can scan me like you scan a box of cereal at the grocery store. But when you scan me, it says where I live and the name of the hospital I visit when I get my shots. On top of all that, I have a doggy bone-shaped steel tag that dangles from my field-dog collar. It says:

American Brittany Rescue

Foster Mom starts spraying me with water and soaping me up with some shampoo that makes my fur fluffy and bright white. That's not a problem. I will have that corrected first thing in the morning. As soon as she lets me outside, I will roll in the dirt and start digging and playing in water so that I can reach that perfect shade of dirty. My Mom likes to scrub and I give her life purpose by getting dirty once again.

I must admit, the best part of my bath is the back rub she gives me. Then she cleans my ears and hand-washes my face before the last rinse of water and thorough drying off with a towel. As soon as she puts me down on the floor, I run through the house, rubbing all the water off my body and on to every piece of furniture, carpet and object available so the whole house smells like me. After I run through the house and have wiped off all the water, my fur starts to dry. It gets curly and looks pretty. Foster Mom takes my special field-dog collar. She removes the bone tag that says, "American Brittany Rescue" off the ring of my collar and places it in a dish on the kitchen countertop. "I don't think you need to wear this anymore, Hedlee."

Tonight, I go into my sleeping box with fluffy fur and I smell like perfume. I feel a little funny because my collar does not have anything dangling from it. There is the brass plate riveted to my collar and the secret chip beneath my skin. Each says I belong to the people who live here, and nothing says that I am a foster dog with a rescue. There has been no ceremony or party or special form filled out. But I don't think I am leaving this ranch in the hills. I hope they keep me. I am entirely happy at the prospect of a forever home. Even with clean, white, curly, smelly fur. ♥ Hedlee

FIFTEEN

#80: DAY 70

My name is Hedlee. Today was the first time I could go on a family outing with all the dog boys. I was so excited, I couldn't contain myself! No, I did not PEE with excitement! Maybe leaked, but not a full-on pee.

We piled into the family wagon and drove to the Mojave Desert, just a fifteen-minute drive from the FARM. Dad put on a vest and wore a hat and carried a string and a toot-toot. The dog boys jumped up and down and ran around. Dad says, "Hunt em up!" but there is nothing to hunt because of a drought. No brush, no birds. He is letting the boys run for exercise. Just the boys! He attached a long rope to my collar. It was the longest leash I ever saw! The dog boys ran free with the air blowing through their ears. They climbed little knolls and peed on every piece of trash and rock they could find. Halfway through the walk, Dad sounded the toot-toot and the boys came running to him. Everyone had water, including me. Then he blew the toot-toot again and they started running again, back to the car.

While I liked seeing the desert, I was sad that I could not run free too. I don't know about the toot-toot and what it means. The boys come when they are called and I am an unknown. I might run away; I might not. Dad says the day that I am better friends with him and the boy dogs is the day I get to run free, with a GPS collar. My new freedom, even if it is running with a fifteen-foot-long leash, is the most I have ever had. Not long ago, I lived on a chain or in a box. My legs are still bowed in such a way that they can't quite straighten out. It makes it hard to run, but I practice in the yard each night. I hope when my legs are straight, I can run without a leash and with freedom. I need straight legs and I want to run and run big. ♥ Hedlee

SIXTEEN

#80: DAY 82

My name is Hedlee. My Foster Mom was reading articles about the days leading up to and after my rescue. As she wiped the water coming from her eyes, this is what she read:

"The next-door neighbor, who has lived next to the dog hoarder for more than three years, said the noise was unbearable at first. He could hear the din over his riding lawnmower. The smell of fecal matter was overpowering and noticeable, even after the dogs were gone. Moreover, the mounds of excrement would attract clouds of flies. The dogs would regularly escape and rummage through his trash because they were hungry."

***

"A righteous man cares for the needs of his animal, but the kindest acts of the wicked are cruel." Saint Francis of Assisi

***

The fact is, we were all hungry and dirty and the smell was unbearable. My fur was matted, ears infected, I had hookworm, and my teeth became black with grime. The breeder broke the

Sacred Vow between Dog and Man. What is "the Sacred Vow," you ask?

We made our vow thousands of years ago, when man domesticated dog. We became man's best friend and working companions in exchange for food, shelter and a place within the family. They say that this vow is Biblically rooted. Dogs do not know about Bibles and certainly cannot quote promises or anything sacred. Dogs don't pray or read, but we inherently know the obligations of dog and man. Some say dogs are messengers of God. I don't know if that is true.

He has not given me a message, or if he did, I may have lost it. I do know for certain I am one of God's beloved creatures.

As legend, has it, the sacred vow between dog and man arose when Saint Francis of Assisi's own voice echoed this truth throughout the land. Some say his word rumbled through the earth and was spoken to babes upon their birth. We hear it rustle in fall leaves and drift softly among all trees. It is faintly heard in the crashing waves, and sometimes echoed from our graves. It is lightly etched upon the finest grain of sand. The word is shared with dog and man. In this vow, he would proclaim, beneath God's own eternal flame, the sacred vow shared from up above; it is not a secret. It is our vow of love.

I promise. ♥ Hedlee

SEVENTEEN

#80: DAY 180

My name is Hedlee. Do dogs dream? Do dogs have hopes and dreams? If you asked me a few months ago, I could not begin to know about hope. My dreams were often a repeat of my day. Dreams are not always good. I had nightmares about bugs, fighting, punishment, food, being tangled, trapped or hurt. Because I did not know any different, I could not see beyond the nightmare, and I accepted this as my fate. With acceptance, there is defeat.

Never in my imagination could I have dreamed of what has happened to me since I moved to a foster home. I can run, super-fast. Freedom is something I cannot describe, but I want it forever. I run, I jump and I feel the wind through my fur as my ears blow behind me. I have food, lots of food. I have dog friends who play with me and don't bite. I have my own sleeping crate. It has a cushion and toys in it and it is my happy box. I have furniture to sit on and games to play, and I have been on family trips. I go swimming. I am starting school. I have been to the ocean. I have chased birds. I have everything a dog could ever want except one thing. A foster home is a temporary home. I have not been adopted.

My crate is in the sleeping room next to where my Foster Mom puts her head on a pillow. When the sky turns dark, she reaches down absentmindedly into the crate and touches my head. I am on my back with my paws in the air, and I smile. While it is hot outside, it is cool in the sleeping room, and I am comfortable. Mom hums me a song while she reads, and I start to dream. I am running on a beach. The ocean water is chasing me while I run after seagulls. I jump, bark and play in the waves. The sea spray is gentle on my face and I feel more than divine. Then I see her. She is standing in the surf, too. I run fast towards the lady who smells like flowers. I jump high into her arms and kiss her face and we fall on the sand together. She laughs. I smile and I dream big.

Dogs do have hopes and dogs do have dreams. I am waiting for mine to come true. Somewhere in my many tomorrows, my forever is waiting to embrace me and it feels something like the beach on a very happy day. ♥ Hedlee

EIGHTEEN
#80: DAY 195

This morning I woke up with an ache in my back, legs and wrist. I took a pretty good tumble yesterday, and now I am paying for it. I awaken with the sniffles, too, and regret opening my eyes. It is still dark out. I open Hedlee's crate. She quickly runs outside with the boy dogs to do her business. Then everyone comes back in and piles onto the bed. We all fall fast asleep. When I stir, I have one dog tucked beneath my arm with her tiny head resting upon my shoulder. She looks up and gently kisses my face. I stroke her fur until I fall back into a contented sleep. She comforts me and lays quietly as my sentry while my body works its restorative magic to get better. Every toss and turn presents a pain with a groan. She stays. I sleep. I heal.

I took this little dog with "issues" in because she needed me. I was wrong. No matter what dog has entered my life, there was always a purpose and eventually a mutual need. The truth is, Hedlee has a purpose. And sometimes, everyone needs a dog like Hedlee. ♥ Magnolia Hedlee's Foster Mom.

NINETEEN

#80: DAY 226

My name is Alice. I am Foster Mom to Magnolia Brittany dog #80, who is also known as Hedlee. I don't know if any of you believe in divine intervention or some bigger plan, but I do, even when it comes to dogs like Hedlee.

The first time I found out about the situation in Louisiana was through some chatter on the Internet. Something "big" was going to happen in the Brittany rescue world, and we needed to be prepared. I honestly had no clue about what was going on, who was involved or when it was going to happen. Then "it" happened. I saw a photo captured from a video taken the day the dogs were seized, an effort now called Operation Magnolia Brittany Rescue. The very first image brought me to complete tears. Tears of sadness; tears of hope; tears for what was and what could be. I told my husband that night about the 103 dogs and the need for foster families all over the United States. I told him I wanted to be a foster. It was the first image on that first day that gave me some sort of purpose, a direction. That decision and direction brought me to my friend Nancy Hensley, whom I have known through field events with the American Kennel Club. Nancy encouraged me to fill out an application for American Brittany Rescue, and I did. I did not know if I would get a Magnolia dog, but I knew I was in line to help a dog, any dog, in need.

After careful background research about our family and home, my application was approved. Many Magnolia dogs were being shipped by transport to California. Most were heartworm positive. I thought a heartworm-positive dog would be too much for my first foster, and Nancy, who is now my foster mentor, agreed. Instead of a Magnolia dog, I was told that there was a need for foster families for some dogs that were being transferred from Colorado to California. I agreed to help, and we waited. I don't know what happened, but I did not get a Colorado dog. Nancy called me instead about one socially challenged, terribly frightened Magnolia dog that needed foster care. My very close friend and neighbor, Janice Gantenbein, is a dog trainer. She agreed to help me with questions and give me guidance with my first foster dog whenever he or she arrived. On Aug. 20, 2013, I met with ABR Coordinator Diana Doiron in Yorba Linda and picked up the most petite and uncharacteristically frightened Brittany I had ever seen. That Brittany is Magnolia Dog #80, who we now know as Hedlee.

We are familiar with the resilience of dogs, particularly the Brittany breed. These are carefree, happy dogs with very good dispositions. Hedlee's true Brittany self was revealed little by little, and with each day we built trust and love. The day she climbed into my lap and fell asleep in my arms was the day I brought her home. My husband looked at me with this vulnerable and sweet dog sleeping in my arms and told me I was going to fail as a foster. He knows me far too well.

I started writing about Hedlee's life, her trials and triumphs not too long after she came to live with us. A couple of weeks ago, I started to do background research for Hedlee's book. I went back to the original newspaper articles leading up to the date the Magnolia dogs were seized. I poured over every video and every newscast, so I could get a complete picture of the events. Finally, I went back to the video I watched the first day I learned of Operation Magnolia Brittany Rescue. It was a complete surprise. The first image that brought me to tears and motivated me to apply as a foster with American Brittany Rescue made me cry again, for a completely different reason.

Image Captured from a Video of Operation Magnolia Brittany Rescue

Remember what I said about divine intervention? The dog on the left is Magnolia dog #80. Her name is Hedlee.

Today I received a call from a man in Antelope Acres. He indicated he was looking for "a little Britt to go huntin' with," and wants to adopt Hedlee. But we all know Hedlee's life and my life were supposed to intersect. I am supposed to write about this dog and she is supposed to be in my life.

The day I took Hedlee home, I made a promise to make certain she has everything she needs and more. She will be clean. She will have her own bed inside her own crate. She will have toys. Her teeth will be brushed. She will have regular veterinary visits. She will go to school. She will even learn to be a field dog. Yes, my husband was right. For once in my life, I am a complete and utter failure. And if American Brittany Rescue will let me, I promise to fulfill my promise to this dog and be the best ~~foster~~ Mom I can be. ♥ Alice

TWENTY
#80: DAY 240

My name is Hedlee. I have been with my foster family a long time now. I think it is because no one wants to adopt me. I have been accepted into this pack, but I don't know if they are MINE. Having something that belongs to me is important. The only thing I am certain of is that I have a bed, a crate and a toy cow named Bessie. I store food in my crate, just in case someone forgets to feed me, which has not happened since I arrived here.

My foster Mom's eyes leak sometimes when she looks at me. I look in those tears and I see a promise and a bond that I have had with no other human. I follow her around the house while she works and she often stops and picks me up and holds me in her arms and kisses my face. I like that.

Today she worked hard. She was tapping her fingers on a square thing and looked at a glowing box on the table when the phone rang. She said my name when she talked, but she was not speaking to me. She walked over to the filing cabinet and picked up a folder that had my name on it and her eyes started leaking, a lot. This worried me as something happened and it involves me. I think I am going to a new home. With this new information, I don't feel confident. She takes out a rubber stamp and presses it on the paper inside my folder. I can't read it. She hangs up the phone and her eyes leak and she makes funny noises until she gets the hiccups. I don't know if she is happy or sad and this is worrisome. I like where I live. I like my box, my bed, Bessie the cow, my dog friends and my Foster Dad. I have even reached an understanding with the cat. Most of all, I like my Foster Mom, even if her eyes leak a little too much.

The next day, Foster Mom prepares for a trip. She put my crate, Bessie and my bed in the car, along with some luggage. She told me to kennel up in the car. This really is the end of my time here. Once everyone is loaded in the car, we travel in the direction of the setting sun, where the air is moist and the wind is soft. We drive through the desert and the mountains to a place where the road meets the sea. We stop at a hotel in Cambria that caters to families with dogs like me. After we check into our room, Foster Mom puts a leash on me and says, "Let's go for a walk, Hedlee." We travel to an off-leash dog beach. For the first time ever, I am permitted to run free, without a leash. It is wonderful. My foster parents smile and laugh while I get chased by waves. I see them smile and hear them say how happy they are that I am going to be with them forever. I am not leaving? Why are we here? I belong to them? They belong to me! "It is a celebration. Hedlee!" said Dad.

I am so happy, I don't know what to do. All I know is I want to remember this moment forever, and I will. Today feels like a dream. The ocean water is chasing me while I run after seagulls. I jump, bark and play in the waves. The sea spray is gentle on my face and I feel more than divine. Then I see them. My parents are standing in the surf, too. I run fast towards the lady who smells like flowers and the man with fur on his face. I jump high into their arms, kiss them, and we all fall on the sand together. Suddenly, it is all real, this life I have always hoped for has now come true. I have a home, my own bed and everyone that I love. I am no longer a foster dog. I am a member of a family. I am adopted!!!

TWENTY-ONE

#80: A NEW YEAR

A New Year gives us the opportunity to examine what went wrong and what went right and how we can improve ourselves for the next 365 days. I don't do resolutions. I just try to be better at wherever it is I fell short. This is not limited to the usual stuff, but to relationships, work and writing. Sometimes we need to renew our commitment, recharge our batteries and, most importantly of all, give thanks for what is good, because appreciation is the key to happiness.

Since August 2013, we have struggled with our girl, Magnolia's Hedlee Lamarr. She survived a tragic youth and was saved when a judge ordered that she and more than a hundred other dogs be seized from a kennel in rural Louisiana. I don't know what happened to her during her first few years of life. I can share now what few knew a year ago, when I was faced with a difficult situation and did not know if I could keep Hedlee. She is afraid of men, and as luck would have it, I am married to a man. The first time she bit him, she thought he was going to take her bone. It is a far stretch to think that. After all, he was a good fifteen feet away from her when he entered the room. She jumped over the couch, ran towards him with gusto and bit him. He was bleeding, and he was mad. The trigger was a dog bone. After the dog bone incident, Hedlee was put in her crate with her bone until she was done with it. During the first few days with a treat in her crate, she seemed happy and content. Then Hedlee noticed that the other dogs were playing while she sat alone in the crate. After a few weeks, the treat became less important and the connection to others became not just a want, but a need. She didn't care about the treats anymore.

By spring of last year, we had settled into a routine, but Hedlee was still overly protective of her pack. Unfortunately, the man of the house was not part of her pack. Each time he left the room, upon return she barked at him viciously…and then again, she bit my husband. The second bite was just as bad as the first, only worse. How could we keep Hedlee if she was aggressive towards my husband? We couldn't. I knew that. I talked to Hedlee's behaviorist (yes, she has one) and worked toward changing her triggers. The dynamics had to change if she was going to get better. This big change involved the man that had nothing to do with her fears but was the trigger, my husband. But would he work with her again, given their unfavorable history? Yes.

Each time my husband entered the room, Hedlee charged him with gusto; she barked, she threatened and she started off mean. Every time she charged, he knelt and played with her and jumped around and acted silly. Annie, our field-trial dog, got in on the game, and soon Annie was wrestling and playing with my husband. What did Hedlee do? She copied Annie. Days turned to weeks and weeks turned to months. Hedlee still barks at imaginary noises, but when my husband enters the room, she runs to him and plays.

We got Hedlee a P.A.L. number last year. "P.A.L." is a purebred alternative listing privilege from the American Kennel Club that will allow Hedlee to compete in events that test her own skills. We wanted her to run in hunt tests, just like our other dogs. When we take Hedlee to the desert, she is a natural hunter. Of course, she is stalking and pointing at tweety birds and not game birds, but she is doing what she is supposed to do, naturally. My husband brought home some farm-raised quail to train the dogs. He took Hedlee to the desert and hid a quail in a bush. When Hedlee approached the bush, the quail flew up and scared her half to death. Hedlee ran back to the car and hid. This is not the act of a bird dog. This is the act of fear. A few weeks ago, we gave it a try again. A quail was hidden in a bush. We took Hedlee running in her normal desert spot. She ran with joy until she got a whiff of the quail. She ran with force, back to the car. I ran back, too. I put a leash on her and brought her to the bird. My husband picked it up and showed it to her. Hedlee did everything she could do to get away from it. Fear from a bad memory. I don't know if Hedlee can ever be a bird dog.

Last night we sat on the couch in a near-dark living room. Hedlee sat next to my husband. Actually, she leaned against him while he rubbed her head. She could hardly keep her eyes open and eventually drifted off to sleep in his arms. This morning we woke up to a new year. I took all the dogs out for their morning constitution. When they ran back in, Hedlee jumped on the bed and started to spit-wash my husband's face. She licked him thoroughly, and he laughed. Then she settled into his arms and they both fell asleep together.

It is a new year and it time to review what has happened, what has not and where we go from here. What I can say is, Hedlee is not going anywhere. She probably won't be a hunting dog, but she is a fine pack member. She loves, she trusts and she has come a long way since 2013. She has joy and freedom and loves her runs in the Mojave Desert. She is happy, playful and has even accepted the dreaded CAT. Most importantly, she has built a relationship with a man who by his gender triggered bad memories. My husband has worked hard to create a good bond and new memories—the kind of memories that give her the courage to lean against him when she needs to and sleep with him because she wants to. In the end, what matters most is that she has and will always have a forever home.

As for New Year's resolutions, I don't do them for a reason. If we work hard at what is important, we don't need them. Real change takes a large helping of courage and often happens slowly. With patience, the rewards for real improvements are greater. Hedlee does not need a New Year's resolution to become a better member of the family. She just needs a little time, nurturing and a dash of courage. We can learn so much from a dog like Hedlee.

Today, while the masses are out huffing and puffing on treadmills, I will be taking a pack of dogs and my husband for a walk in the Mojave Desert. We will have fun and joy and will connect with nature. In the weeks and months to come, we will soak Hedlee's favorite toy with quail scent. She will graduate to a feather and will eventually be reintroduced to birds. Time heals all wounds. What can we learn from Miss Hedlee Lamarr? Sometimes we must let go of the past in order to embrace the future. For all who have lived through the bad, it is time to let it go. You can't move forward if you are always looking back. You deserve a better you.

Hedlee did not know she had dreams until she found out what it meant to dream. With a peek at her future and a wave to her past, the future she will stay with, because it will always last.

TWENTY-TWO
#80: HAPPY RESCUE-VERSARY

My special name is Magnolia's Hedlee Lamarr's Happily Ever After. "Magnolia" is the name of the operation that rescued 103 dogs in rural Louisiana. But "Magnolia" has many other meanings. A magnolia tree is strong and the blooms on the tree come in a variety of colors, each with a different meaning. A pink magnolia flower symbolizes innocence; white is purity; green is joy; purple is truth. Then there is the steel magnolia, for those who are strong as steel and rise above hardships. A Magnolia dog is pure joy, filled with innocence and truth. We have overcome and triumphed over our past, which makes us steel-magnolia strong. I am Hedlee and I am a Magnolia dog; but today, I am so much more than my past. I am the member of a family. I am a friend. I am 30 pounds of pure love. I don't remember my past life because my new life is so good. I am Hedlee and I represent a rainbow of magnolia flowers because I have done more than survive. Because of Operation Magnolia Brittany Rescue, I have thrived.

TWENTY-THREE

#80: HEDLEE'S VALENTINE

Today, we witnessed a miracle. But first, I feel as though I have lied to everyone. Not a true fib as defined by Webster's. What I mean is the absence of the truth, which is not quite a fib, but an omission. My life is an open book. But this time, I could not say what we were about to do. We could fail. If we failed, would I tell you? Eventually. I would tell you. Eventually.

This morning we took our time getting ready. I stayed in bed and hugged Hedlee while my husband, Jay, watched fishing shows. Eventually I rolled out of bed, took a shower and put on some jeans and boots. Before we headed to the desert, we took Hedlee to Jack's Place for breakfast. We dined on the patio. She enjoyed her scrambled eggs and we watched the sleepy town of Leona Valley wake up to a beautiful and unseasonably warm Valentine's Day.

We drove just outside California City, exited at Clay Mine Road and headed north. Asphalt turned to dirt and dirt mixed with sand as we made our way to the hunt-test grounds shared by the California and San Diego Brittany clubs. A double-double hunt test was scheduled for today. We arrived just as lunch was being served and let Hedlee watch the people as they ate. Someone even gave her a treat. "Is that the rescue?" "Yes. We entered her in one brace."

Hedlee was part of Operation Magnolia Brittany Rescue, which involved the court ordered seizure of 103 Brittany dogs. Hedlee is dog #80. When she came to us more than two years ago, she was afraid of people and she was a fear biter. It took eighteen months for her to warm up to my husband and now their bond is unbreakable. But the fear of strangers and her environment continued to plague her mind. She even carried a fear of game birds, specifically, quail. Hedlee is fine with wild birds and will point at the meadowlark that grace the fields of our small town. But the piece of her past that included quail was a frightening one. When we walked passed the bird pen today, I was relieved to see chukar, a member of the partridge family. No quail.

For the first time in Hedlee's life, I put a brace collar on her neck. A brace collar allows an American Kennel Club judge to identify a dog by the color of the collar. Hedlee wore orange, and her brace-mate, a young and playful German Shorthaired Pointer, wore yellow. Today, my husband Jay would be responsible for handling Hedlee. I received permission to walk in the gallery and carried my camera to witness whatever might happen. Jay looked back at me and I nodded my head as he released her from her leash. Hedlee was not sure what she should do and neither of us were sure as to what she might do. We expected her to run back to the car. She ran forward. Then she turned around and ran back toward camp. Jay called her, and she turned around and ran with uncertainty in her step towards the gently rolling desert terrain. She continued to run forward at least temporarily, without fear. Each time fear took over, she turned around and ran in the wrong direction. It was a constant tug and pull. Nature versus fear. Eventually, nature took over and Hedlee made it to the bird field.

I thought I heard wrong when someone said, "She is on point!" I looked in disbelief. She needed to hold that point for three seconds. I stared and forgot to pick up my camera. Tears started streaming down as I lifted the camera to my face. I could not see what I was photographing because my glasses fogged up. Jay repeated, "I got a point." He gently kicked the bush, the bird flew up and he shot his blank gun into the sky. Hedlee flinched and became skittish. She ran backwards and considered taking herself back to camp. Jay called her and walked away from the bush that had previously held the bird. He called to her again and again. Finally, she joined his side. The clock stopped. We did not know if she passed or failed, but we were happy because she tried. Best of all, she pointed at a bird. We knew we just witnessed a miracle. A thirty-pound, white and orange, beautiful, fuzzy miracle.

How many of us are survivors of something horrible? Who has suffered a terrible childhood? A loss? Lived through cruelty? The unimaginable? Let's face it. We all have gone through something. Hedlee has shown us all that no matter how bad life has been, we can rise above it and become better than our past. Hedlee is not just a survivor. Hedlee faced her fear head on with bravery, and she pointed at it. And today, she was rewarded for her courage with an orange ribbon from the California Brittany Club along with a lot of tears and cheers. Of all the ribbons our dogs have earned over the years, the Junior Hunter ribbon Hedlee earned today has made us proudest.

TWENTY-FOUR
FRED, PART I

My name is Fred Benoit. I am writing this as a public service to my fellow Brittany dogs who may become victims of what I perceive to be a vast conspiracy against good dogs like me.

Like I said, I am a pretty good boy. I eat my vitamins, sleep quietly next to my humans without taking up too much space on the bed, and I exercise to stay fit. Sure, I steal an occasional meal off the countertop; and yes, I have taken bones and treats from other dogs. But does that mean that I should become a victim?

Yesterday, my Mom took me before breakfast time to get a pedicure and a manicure. Pedi's and mani's? I am ALL in! She drops me off and says she loves me and I think great, she will pick me up in a couple of hours and we will go fetch a burger. Next thing I know, I am put in a cage and then people start poking and prodding at me. I have been kidnapped! Right here on American soil! I have rights! I am a GOOD canine citizen! Hey, what about the Geneva Convention? I need food! I need a reasonable amount of space.

Panic sets in as I contemplate how to escape. Then they knock me out. I mean WHAMMO! When I wake up, I am back in the wire box, drooling. I don't feel right. I have been drugged. Two teeth are missing. I look…down. OMG! My balls are gone! They're GONE!!! I am so snockered on whatever drug they gave me, I can't even bark. I fall asleep. When I wake up, it seems to me that it is early evening. I am not quite sure, as I have lost all concept of time. Then I see my teacher, Janice, who is also a close family friend. I want to shout: "Janice! Help!" But there she is, hanging out with the man that kidnapped and conducted dastardly experiments on me. She says something, but I don't understand. It sounds like, "blah blah blah blah." Then she LEAVES me in the cage! I silently cry. Oh Janice. Why have your forsaken me? Et tu, Janice?

I don't know how long I wait or what has happened. I sleep; I wake, and I think about how hungry I am. Many hours have passed since my abduction. I want to cry, but I am tired so I just moan and wait. I don't know if it is hours or days, but suddenly I hear noises. People. Activity. I am going to be RESCUED!!! I hear my Mommy. I want to shout "Mommy, come get me!" But my throat is parched, and I don't have the energy. I hear her talking to people. She is paying the ransom so that I can be released. Someone comes and opens my box, pulls a needle out of my arm and tells me to march. I march. I pull and race to the person I trust most. Mommy! I am coming home! She hugs and kisses me and takes me home. I am fed scrambled eggs. But the ordeal does not end there. I am now crowned with the cone of shame and I think there are drugs in my food. Et tu, Mommy?

Don't let this happen to you.

Yours truly,
Fred Benoit

TWENTY-FIVE
FRED, PART II

I guess everybody knows that I was kidnapped and tortured the other day. They castrated me, pulled out some teeth and put me in a cage without food. My Mom paid the ransom and I am home recovering from the terrible ordeal.

This morning I woke up and I felt more like myself. Sleeping next to me is the girl of my dreams, Annie. Her fur is soft and white and she is always happy. Annie is releasing pheromones, which means she might reciprocate my advances. I smell her butt, she smells mine. She does not seem to mind that I am wearing the cone of shame. Today, I wear it as a badge of honor. It shows I am a survivor. I was held hostage and now I am free to live a good life, with Annie. She smiles, she jumps and then she grabs the cone of shame in her teeth! Her teeth! She starts tugging and pulling and dragging me around by the cone. I am FORCED into Annie's world of fun. I am her toy, and NOT in a good way. She shakes my cone like it is a dead animal, and my head shakes along with it. Then, the cone breaks. This is true shame. Don't let this happen to you.

Your humiliated friend,
Fred Benoit

TWENTY-SIX

LOST AND FOUND

The last thing he wanted to hear on a Saturday night. "He's gone, I can't find him." Jay looked up from his study book. "Wasn't he with the other two boys? Maybe he is hiding?" But Fred was not hiding. He was missing. I looked through the house and I searched the entire yard. Our smallest Brittany had disappeared. Jay grabbed his flashlight and his field-dog whistle and started hiking around the neighboring properties.

Since they were small pups, all our dogs have been trained to the sound of a whistle. A blast of a whistle means "come here," and Fred is the most obedient of them all. If Fred hears a whistle, he comes running, no matter how far he must run. After the first half hour of calls and shrill whistling, Fred did not return to our side. It was clear that he was truly lost.

I took my Avalon and headed west on Leona Avenue while Jay headed east in the Scion. We drove up and down private driveways yelling "Fred!" followed by a loud whistle call. Nothing. I drove up hillsides and down canyons to the far end of town. I stopped the car and listened. All I heard was the jubilant celebration of a pack of coyotes as they enjoyed a wintertime feast. I started to cry. Living in wild country is quite beautiful, but this stunning beauty is filled with risks to a dog.

Coyotes, mountain lions, fast cars, poison, any number of hazards could take our little boy. I don't know what I would do if he were hurt... or killed. And now, a full hour has passed. Our property is only a few lots away from the Angeles National Forest. He may never be found.

While I thought the worst, Jay did not panic. He went back home. Knowing that Fred is not a fence jumper, Jay reexamined the property one more time. He searched around the temporary home thoroughly and then faintly heard clink, clink, clink, the sound of Fred's identification tags hitting against each other. Fred was trapped beneath the house and did not know how to get out. Upon opening the trap door to the side of the house, the light of the flashlight shined through the darkened place. A frightened dog covered in dirt and dust crouched far away. "Come here Fred!" Cautious at first, Fred knew to leave the darkness and follow the stream of welcoming light. And when he did, he found his way back to the safe arms that he always loved.

Many of us search high and low for the meaning of life. We often do this by conquering a great task, going on a fantastic voyage, purchasing a fast car, climbing the biggest mountain or finding our way to a mysterious land. We travel far and wide, over land and sea, never realizing that what is most important and what gives us the most meaning is in the place we are least likely to look. At first glance, "it" seems to be illusive if not missing. But if we look real hard and listen quite carefully, we will find that the search for what truly matters was never far away. It is not in a canyon, a valley, on a hillside or in a forest. It was never in a mysterious far away land. In the end, you will discover that your life has meaning and what you were seeking was never truly lost. It has always been and will always be beneath the shingled roof with a flickering glow of a fire at the most welcoming place on God's green earth...a place we all call home.

Welcome home, Fred. You were never lost. We were.

TWENTY-SEVEN
BUDDY, FRED & HEDLEE

Last night I was restless, worried about someone I love. Eventually, I crawled into bed exhausted, and willed myself to sleep. An hour later, Fred scratched at the bedroom door. He wanted me to take him out. He acted as though he had to go potty, when we all know that Fred the forager was seeking any hidden treasure that might be found beneath the midnight sky. I opened the door and Fred, Hedlee and Buddy went single file out the door. I followed them.

The moon was full and glorious, the crickets chirped with delight as our resident owl was standing guard high on a branch in our big-cone pine tree. Sometimes I forget the place we call home is like a dream. I scan the darkened landscape as Hedlee, Fred and Buddy return to the shelter of our home and settle in for the night.

Fred looks inside Hedlee's crate for non-existent treats while Buddy struggles with rearranging his bed just right. Hedlee jumps up on our bed, gives me a hug and kiss, and then creeps slowly and carefully to my soundly sleeping husband, gently touching his face with her nose before curling up in a ball for the remainder of the night. I take my spot on the south side of the bed, next to my snoring husband. I watch his chest move up and down. His face is silhouetted by the moonlight and in that gentle glow I am reminded of how much I love this man.

In a few paragraphs, one can see I have so much to be thankful for during one single night. I am thankful for the full moon, a sky filled with stars, the sound of crickets and the hoot of an owl. I am blessed to live in a place that I could never have imagined as a child. The bounty of its beauty is truly a dream come true. I am glad for the shelter I live within, as modest as it is, and I am blessed to have a comfortable place to rest my head after working and writing and being. I am thankful for the bond and trust I have with a rescued dog that continues to overcome her past and is now kissing her future. I am thankful for the time I have with a man I have known for decades and I am glad for the life, love and dreams we have built together.

TWENTY-EIGHT
ANNIE'S JOURNEY HOME

Annie was born on our wedding anniversary. Today, she is five years old. Little does she know that she is going to have quite a celebration. The day we took her home, she was a wild one. Here is an excerpt that I wrote about that day (and happy birthday, Annie).

In Annie's own words:

When my new parents drove me home from Texas, I was a good girl for the first half of the trip. I did not reveal my true self until we arrived in Flagstaff, Arizona. We stayed at a nice hotel. The lobby was covered in marble and fancy paintings. Honestly, it was a bit hoity-toity for my liking. My parents took me to go potty before we checked into the hotel, but I was too busy smelling everything to worry about doing my business. My Mom signed her life away during check-in and claimed I was a "good" girl even though she had just met me. The hotel staff hugged me and agreed that I was a good girl, so there was no extra charge for me to stay at the fancy establishment. Mom and Dad took me upstairs to the beautiful room. As soon as they put me on the floor, I spotted the luxurious, floor-to ceiling-velvet drapes. I ran across the room, jumped high in the air, clamped my teeth halfway up the soft fabric and swung like

Tarzan. As my parent's eyes bulged with what appeared to be shock, I jumped from the drapes, ran to the middle of the room and squatted out the biggest turd ever. They realized I was not exactly a good girl, but laughed and loved me anyway.

And I love them too.

TWENTY-NINE
JUST A DOG

I am just a dog. I gladly pee and poop outside. I find it appalling when you pee and poop in my porcelain water bowl. But what do I know? I am just a dog.

I am just a dog. I sit, stay and shake your hand on command. But when someone tells you what to do, you don't listen. But what do I know? I am just a dog.

I am just a dog. I am a leader, not a follower. I can move a flock of sheep into a designated area while you admire my God-given talent. I have never seen a human round up a flock without the aid of an animal...except in church. But what do I know? I am just a dog.

I am just a dog. I have a keen sense of smell that guides me to that bird in the bush. I stand and I point while you kick the bird out of the bush and it flies. It lands far away, but I bring it back to your hand and you act like you were the one that found and brought it back. But what do I know? I am just a dog.

I am just a dog. I can find a varmint in a hidden area just by listening and smelling. Meanwhile, you hire someone to find them for you. But what do I know? I am just a dog.

I am just a dog. I have great speed and agility. I hunt by sight and by speed and can overtake prey with my tremendous endurance. You purchase your "prey" at the grocery store. But what do I know? I am just a dog.

I am just a dog. I provide comfort to those who are weak, and I am a companion to those who are lonely. I visit the sick in hospitals and the lonely in the senior center while most of you are too busy to do so. But what do I know? I am just a dog.

I am just a dog. I am ready to work when disaster strikes. I am here to find the living beneath the rubble. I am your eyes, ears and nose. If there is a heartbeat, I will find it. But what do I know? I am just a dog.

I am just a dog. I am here to protect and to serve. I can overtake a bad guy and hold him until you arrive. I do so without a gun. Just my wit, my strength and bravery keep you out of harm's way. We are a team. To you, I am not just a dog. I am your partner.

I am just a dog. I am your friend. We like to play together, eat together and sleep together. You give me your treats, even when I don't share mine. I have been with you when you were sick, lost and mournful. I have been with you for each and every joy; throughout every single season. To you, I am not invisible. I am someone you love and I love you, too. And when the day comes when you lay me to rest, you will never say I was "just a dog," for you and I both know our relationship is so much more than human and dog. I am not just a dog. I am your family.

THIRTY
HOLLY

I am a researcher by nature and have always been fascinated by odd facts and figures. For example, to walk from my house to Leona Valley Elementary School is exactly 7,118 feet. My stride is typically three feet in length, which means it takes me approximately 2,373 steps to reach the corner of 90th and Leona Avenue—that is, if I don't take Ralph. Ralph is my very regal, nine-year-old German Shepherd. He is not interested in short cuts or a direct route. No, he needs to complete switchbacks between the north and south sides of Leona Avenue, smelling every tree, telephone pole and gopher hideaway in or out of our path. When we finally arrive home, he returns to his job of guarding our five goats and Holly, our beautiful Brittany.

We found Holly at a rescue and thought she would be a perfect fit as a hunting dog. Her first day out in the field, she fell into a small ravine instead of jumping over it. It turns out Holly has several birth defects, along with the rest of the litter. She is the last to survive. She, too, is nine years old, but has very little fur, no eyes. Her bark is an odd sort of grunt and her body is riddled with tumors. Holly does not leave the homestead very often except for her regular veterinarian care. But this does not stop her enthusiasm for wanting to be like the other dog. Tonight, I came home and looked at Holly's blank face. Much to Ralph's chagrin, Holly left with a leash and with me.

Although she is sightless, Holly is a leader. She cautiously led me to the asphalt roadway, turned right and headed east, as if she has walked this way a million times before. Unlike Ralph, she has a purpose to her step and a goal, to go straight and enjoy all the interesting smells and the breeze. No switchbacks; she happily guides me like a champion to the corner of 90th and Leona Avenue, 2,373 steps, then we turn around and she leads me back home.

Even though Holly has no eyes, she knows where she is going, and in blindness, she can lead her sighted companion home. The same holds true for people. Often in life we have personal disabilities, but we have other talents that can compensate for our shortcomings. Using alternative skills, the blind can lead the sighted. If Holly can do it, I know we can, too.

THIRTY-ONE
THE BLIND LEADING

Today I walked my blind, nine-year-old Brittany with an immune disorder down the sandy dirt path that runs along the main thoroughfare of my town, Leona Valley. She is oblivious to her latent defects as she trots ahead, leading her person companion briskly on this crisp spring morning. Meanwhile, I, with so many blessings, often feel compelled to focus acutely on my own deficiencies in a uniquely human fashion. I believe I can learn so much from this jovial little creature called a dog.

We follow the fence lines down the street as curious horses seek to greet us as we pass by each small ranch. The cold air slaps my face and my eyes squint as I scan the hues of white and pink blossoms from the cherry and pear trees that dot the flatlands and hillsides of this quaint small town. Motorists who are strangers to me wave as they drive by, and I reciprocate with a hardy wave and a smile. Puffy cumulous clouds threaten to dampen this journey, but I do not care. I look down at my elated pet, her entire snout now fully inserted into a gopher hole as her tail sways rapidly back and forth, and I unequivocally know I have finally found the closest place to heaven on earth.

THIRTY-TWO
THE BEST DOG

Throughout my life, I have had some wonderful dogs. The first "best dog I ever had" was a hunting dog, a German Shorthaired Pointer. My Dad gave her a name indicative of her country of origin, "Sigrid Von Deutsch Hound". For some reason, that name did not stick with us kids. We just called her "Puppy."

Puppy was solid liver in color with a spot of white on her chest. She was tolerant of us while we dressed her in clothing, placed hats on her head or climbed upon her back like she was a horse. But her most defining role in our home happened while we were fast asleep. A man was in our backyard and had readied to climb through my bedroom window when Puppy came from behind and attacked him with everything she had. The man turned and kicked her and kicked her hard. Then the coward ran away. Puppy was found next to our lemon tree with broken ribs and a collapsed lung. Her life was slipping away.

This happened in the early 1970s. My parents were quite poor and did not have enough money to keep shoes on our feet, but still they rushed our hero Puppy to the vet for emergency surgery, and somehow, she survived. That next week she came home and there was so much to celebrate. My grandparents were in town, there were presents under the Christmas tree and our hero dog was home!

I was always particularly close to my grandfather, a fastidious man with quiet temperament. I remember him in his white button-front dress shirt and tie as we climbed into the back seat of his new car for a ride on that sunny Christmas morning. When we came home, we found Puppy in a pool of blood, for she had ripped out most of her stitches. Grandfather, the man who long declared his dislike of dogs, quickly wrapped Puppy in a blanket. The blood soaked through to his white dress shirt as he carried her to his new car. He broke all the rules as he raced her to the veterinary hospital. Time ticked by and we did not know if Puppy would ever come home. The house was silent for the remainder of the day as we sat quiet and worriedly waited for the inevitable.

Late in the afternoon, my grandfather returned and parked his new car neatly against the curb. I was afraid of what could be. Yet still we children pressed our noses to the divided glass windows of our house on Jersey Street. My grandpa climbed out of his shiny car with freshly ruined upholstery. The large quantity of dried blood on his shirt seemed to tell the sad story of the beginning and the end of the hero dog named Puppy. Grandpa stood up straight, stretched and breathed a heavy sigh. Then he turned and opened the rear car door, bent over, and gently picked up our newly re-stitched Puppy.

Puppy lived many happy years as our favorite family dog. Ironically, Grandpa passed away exactly two decades to the day he saved the life of Puppy. The man who rescued Christmas left us on Christmas. Just like you, he is a treasured gift that I shall never, ever forget.

***

Postscript to this story: As for my grandfather and his legendary distaste for dogs, today I shall call it a myth. Recently, I was looking at some old photographs of my mother as a little girl with her first "best" dog she ever had. One of many photos I found was like this picture dated June 1943, featuring Mom, Grandma Bernice and their springer spaniel, Ricky. Looking at the camera, the pair and their canine companion appear to be content. Each one is full of so much promise and hope. And I assure you, the man who took the picture was likely wearing his signature button-front white dress shirt with tie. And while looking through the camera lens at his wife, his three-year-old daughter and his beloved dog, he most assuredly was smiling.

THIRTY-THREE

GRIZZLY

At the end of this book, a dog dies. There is no need to skip to the last page to find out what happened in advance. He is dead. I can tell you that because it already happened. It was his destiny. Yes, we all have a fate that includes birth and death, but his death came far too soon and somehow, we knew it would happen. I remember when Grizz was a young dog and my husband and I had already fallen deeply in love with him. Grizz was doing something funny, and suddenly, my husband had tears in his eyes. Now mind you, my husband is a six-foot-three-inch, very masculine plumber. Without asking him, I already knew what he was thinking. Grizzly was not going to live to be an old dog. I don't know how we knew, but we did. It was his fate. Now our Grizzly is buried lovingly beneath the shade of a cottonwood tree. Each fall, the quail cross his path and hide in a bush near his grave. When Grizz was alive, he loved to sit on top of the patio table at night, enjoying a panoramic view of Leona Valley. His final resting place still enjoys that view.

I have had an intimate relationship with grief for the last eighteen months. It weighed me down and practically dragged my very being into the grave with Grizzly. I don't know how I functioned. I faked it. I put on a smile and went to work as if nothing were wrong while the inside of me felt like jelly. I woke up, went to work, came home and went to sleep; then I started all over again. The worst part was the guilt. Did I do something wrong? Could I have prevented the outcome? The "what ifs" swam constantly in my brain.

A couple of years prior to Grizzly's death, a dog-food sales representative at PetSmart tried to talk me out of buying dog food X. If I bought brand X, my dog would die of cancer, just like her dog. If I bought brand Y, I would save my dog. She was so adamant about it, she started crying right there on Aisle 3. I didn't know what to do. Brand X, a very expensive brand with good ingredients, had not been recalled. I had not heard that Brand X caused cancer, yet there I was with a sales rep and she was crying hysterically, convinced that she could have saved her dog from dying if she purchased Brand Y. Believe me, this conversation came back to haunt me a few years later, when Grizzly was diagnosed with pancreatic cancer. What if I had bought Brand Y. What if?

I also considered where I live, in a farm town in rural northern Los Angeles County. My mini-ranch is downhill from old orchards that have occupied this land from the 1920s to the present. One old orchard I knew was treated with dangerous pesticides that today are illegal. I thought about Grizzly. If you know anything about Brittanys, they are diggers. They love to create holes and tunnels. If there was a champion of champions in the digging department, it was Grizz. When he was done, our place looked like an archeological site once occupied by ancient treasure rather than gophers and squirrels. All those holes. What if the soil was contaminated? What if?

A "what if" that hit our veterinarian hard was the full blood panel we had completed for Grizz a year before he passed. Everything was perfect except for a false positive reading on his sugar levels. When Grizzly's test came back as what was perceived as clean, we took him on a trip throughout the Western United States. He had the best time of his life. If there was a hint that he had cancer, we would have never taken him on that trip. And because it was pancreatic cancer, the treatment has a high failure rate. If we had known, we would have watched Grizz like a hawk and he would not have enjoyed his last year. I am glad we did not know. I think Grizzly is probably glad, too. That is more than fate; that is divine intervention.

We can all worry about the "what ifs" in our life, but "what if" does not change what has already happened. We can learn and improve from our mistakes, but we cannot change the past. I do not regret the food I fed my dog or where we live. As for the holes and the mazes he left behind, that was his joy. Could I really take that away from him? No. Just like I am glad I did not know he had cancer before his big adventure. The most important part of life is living and that is exactly what he did. Grizzly lived and in our small world he lived big.

THIRTY-FOUR
GRIZZLY: NOT READY

I am startled out of a nightmare. Gasping, I sit up straight, look over my husband's side of the bed and see Grizzly is still alive, his chest is lifting up and down. He is silent in his slumber. I start to cry. My husband reaches for me and rubs my back. "Don't cry" is all he says. My arms hurt. I have had the same dream each night since January 13. Some force is trying to take my best dog away. I hold onto Grizzly with all my might. My muscles tense and shake. It hurts, but I hold on tighter. I am not going to let him go. I wake up again and again to check to see if he is still breathing. Grizzly is dying of pancreatic cancer.

We know that Grizzly only has days, perhaps weeks, to live. We want to make sure that whatever happens, each day is his best. We take him on short excursions that awaken his senses and remind him that he is a field dog. His energy is depleted, so these trips are very short. Last night we took him to Ritter Ranch, a place that was once a thriving cattle ranch, but now is overgrown and filled with wildlife. I open the car door and Grizzly jumps down. I want to walk him on the leash but my husband says, "Let him go." I worry. He might fall and get hurt. His legs are weak. I want him at my side. "I would rather have him run this field and die than wait at home to die." I consider my husband's wisdom, detach Grizzly's leash and let him go.

Grizzly's nose wiggles, and he smiles. He walks quickly with a wobbly gait to each bush, hole and tree. He does so with caution because he, too, knows he is not strong. He studies each slope and determines if he can climb it, and sometimes he stops and turns the other way. Towards the end of his journey, he walks closely behind us, until our pace evolves into a slow crawl. As the winter sun sets, I open the car door, but Grizzly is too frail to jump inside. My husband gently picks him up and places him on the car seat with harness, and we return to our humble home.

Since his diagnosis, Grizzly is with me 24/7. He is hypoglycemic and requires small meals every few hours. I crush his vitamins into his homemade food. Tonight, he is exhausted. My husband calls him to bed. Soon, Grizzly is on his back, legs in the air and they are kicking. I know he is dreaming of his evening at the ranch. I slide into bed and start to drift into sleep. My arms tense, the grip of my fingers tightens until my nails gouge into my hands. When I wake up, he might be gone. In my sleep, I hold on tighter. I wake up again and see that he is still alive. I know that soon, my grip will waiver, my strength will fail and Grizzly will slip away.

Sometimes, because we love them, we must let them go...

And with broken hearts, we did.

THIRTY-FIVE

THE COLOR ORANGE

My name is Grizzly. I am a good boy. When I was a puppy, there was a choosing ceremony. A man and his wife came to the ranch. I played with the man's shoelaces. He picked me up and I rested my head on his shoulder. Then I hugged him. He turned his head to the woman who would become my mother and said, "I want this one." I was the only puppy in the litter with a name because I was the pick of the litter. My name has always been Grizzly. I chose my Dad and he chose me.

I am a bird dog. I like to point at birds. I like to carry birds in my mouth and I love to give them to my Dad. When I was a teenager, my Dad took me to classes to learn how to be a hunting dog. I was very shy and did not do well in class. Everyone watched me and it bothered me so I did not hunt. One day the teacher placed a bird in front of me and released the bird. The teacher told my Dad, "Release your dog." Dad took me off my lead and said, "Hunt-em up, Grizzly!" I ran after that bird. As I ran, the rest of the world disappeared. It was just me and the bird. We were both flying away. I ran a good mile into the stark Mojave Desert. I was a speck on the horizon and the class could barely see me through binoculars. Then I turned and made a mad run back. I ran with force, with the wind in my fur and the sun on my back. I ran with joy, with freedom and with a sense of purpose. You could have heard a pin drop when I placed the live game bird in the palm of my father's hand. He was so proud when he handed the bird back to the teacher, without a drop of spit. I had the longest retrieve and the softest mouth. I have always been a good boy.

I was ready for my first hunting test. It was a lot of fun. I cleared the field of birds and my Dad had so many birds he was handing them to the judges because he could not carry any more. The judge from Arizona jumped off his horse and shook my Dad's hand, thanking him for bringing me to the hunt test. I was the best dog he ever saw. My first test as a Junior Hunter, I scored all tens. My last test as a Master Hunter, I scored all tens. My Dad was proud of me. I am a good boy.

I am a handsome Brittany. I have a big block head, a square, muscular body and a saddle of orange on my back and sides. My Aunt, who is also my obedience teacher, sent my picture in to a company and they liked me. Then she took me to Smashbox Studios in Hollywood and I became a super model. I was good enough to grace the cover of a bag of dog food for an international company, then modeled for a different brand of dog food two years later. I was called back because I am handsome, I follow instructions and I am a good boy.

A year ago, I lost ten pounds. I was fifty pounds and then, all of a sudden, I was forty pounds. I am an active dog and I like to run a lot. Lots of tests were run and repeated but nothing showed up. My parents bought me special food to help me gain weight, but I never did. Then they took me on a trip and I went all over the western United States. I have been to Washington, Oregon, Nevada, Idaho and throughout California. I have run in the deserts of California, Idaho and Oregon. My paws have touched the glacier waters of the high Sierra and I have walked the sandy beaches from Cambria to Malibu. I have gone on these trips because I am loved and because I am a good boy.

In January, I got very sick. My parents took me to the emergency room because my legs were shaking uncontrollably. I was having a hypoglycemic attack. The next day I went to see a special doctor and he took pictures of the inside of my body. The pictures showed that I have lots of tumors. It is cancer. The cancer started in my pancreas and spread to my stomach and liver. One big tumor pushed on my heart. My parents were told I had two weeks to live. They cried because they love me and because I am a good boy.

After I was diagnosed, my parents tried to recreate the best days of my life. They took me to lakes, the desert and the beach. I even went hunting and carried a bird for the last time. When I could no longer run, my Mom put bird feeders in front of the window and the quail came and ate right next to me. I stared at them and wiggled my nose and remembered the days when I carried them in my mouth.

I lived much longer than the two-week prediction. After two months, I was still doing fine. Then, a couple weeks later, I got really sick. I could not eat, and when I did, I had diarrhea. My Dad was recovering from surgery, so my Mom went outside to dig my grave. I sat next to her while she dug a big hole. The deeper she dug the more interested I became in the process. I started to dig, too. Soon, we were both digging together. I was digging for a squirrel and she was digging and crying, until she noticed what I was doing. Then she started to laugh. It was not time for me to go, so the grave remained empty for two more weeks. The only thing in that grave was my Mom's dried tears and the echoes of her laughter, because I am a good boy.

On what would be my last full day, my Mom took me to the lake. I love the lake. There are lots of birds, bunnies and lizards. She walked me a short distance and saw that I was tired so we went back to the car. She drove me slowly around the lake, with the windows down, so I could smell everything that I love. When we got home, my right eye rolled backwards because a tumor was pushing on my optic nerve. The cancer had gone to my brain. The next morning, I was completely blind and I was scared. My Dad carried me the same way he did the day he brought me home. I rested my head on his shoulder and hugged him. He placed me in the car and rolled down the windows so that I could smell the horses, cows and birds. He drove me to the place where I took obedience classes, the place where I first learned to be a good boy. My uncle works there and gave me a sedative. My eyes returned to normal and suddenly I could see that bird I chased when I was a teenager. It flew in front of me. Then I heard the teacher say, "Release your dog." Then I remembered what my Dad had said so long ago, "Hunt'em up, Grizzly!" As I ran, the rest of the world disappeared. It was just me and that bird. I chased that bird into the sky. I ran with force, with the wind in my fur and the sun on my back. I ran with joy, with freedom and with a sense of purpose. I was a young dog again, strong, bold and handsome. I am and have always been a good boy. I ran to the place where rainbows are made. After each rain, look at the rainbow in the sky. I am the color orange.

R.I.P. Grizzly Discoveries, Master Hunter, aka Grizzly Benoit, August 4, 2005-April 1, 2014

If you liked the story of Grizzly, you are welcome to share it with your friends. This is a reprint of my Facebook post from April 4, 2014.

www.facebook.com/photo.php?fbid=10202533203543811

THIRTY-SIX

GRIEF

We lost our dog Grizzly to pancreatic cancer a month ago, as of the date of this writing. I have cried each day since he died. I told my husband that it hurts as much today as it did a month ago. He nodded his head solemnly with tears in his eyes and said, "I know."

It took me a month to visit his grave. Grizzly was put down at the vet while I was at work. My husband drove him back home to our small farm. He wrapped him in a blanket and placed quail feathers on him inside his grave. My husband buried him alone. I can't even imagine how hard this was for him. He wanted to spare me from this process. For thirty days, I could not look in the direction of Grizzly's burial plot. If I looked, I guess it would seem more real. Yesterday, I visited Grizzly's grave. A small mound of dirt bordered by carefully placed granite rocks marks the spot of our beloved boy. I cried as if he died yesterday. I did not cry alone.

It is odd how we treat the death of a dog. It is almost taboo to mourn their passing. Employers often give a few days off to grieve the loss of an immediate family member, but when the immediate family member is a dog, there is no time to grieve. It is the family dog who is with us for a morning or evening walk.

They sleep in our homes, go on vacations and are beside us with the flicker of the television before we fall asleep. A dog is there for our triumphs and failures and all of life's frailties.

A few days after Grizzly died, I wrote about the life of the dog boy we lost. My sorrow was still fresh, as well as my joy and love for my best dog friend. The story of our orange and white Brittany was shared throughout the world and translated into several languages. I received condolences from hundreds of people whom I did not know. They all have loved and lost their own and shared in our grief. Each one cried for a dog they did not know who lived in a town they never visited with people they never met. The day Grizzly died, I could count on two hands those who shed a tear. Without exaggeration, one week later, thousands cried.

I have had some time to think about what has transpired. Those strangers shared in our tears because they have suffered a loss, too. Except "loss" is not exactly the correct word. It is that we are now missing a love that was pure and deep and true. In reality, because of a dog we have each gained so much. Most of us have become better people. In the burial of Grizzly, I found something I was not expecting to find…. Humanity.

THIRTY-SEVEN
TWO MONTHS

As we near the end of the second month without Grizzly, I must say it has been beyond difficult. Whatever level of dread we had anticipated with his expected loss, the reality was much worse than we could have ever imagined. A couple days ago, I sat on the couch looking out the window that Grizzly loved to look out, watching the quail call others for food beneath the feeders. I looked out beyond what would have been Grizzly's normal line of sight, and noticed my husband standing over Grizzly's grave. He leaned with one hand pressing against a cottonwood tree that canopies the grave, the other hand hanging down like a weight, his shoulders stooped and his face angled downward and etched with pain. We felt the exact thing at the exact same time, but we were not physically with each other when it happened. But I saw, and I knew and I wept.

We both really miss our good boy.

THIRTY-EIGHT
DIGGING

My good boy Grizzly took his journey over the rainbow bridge. As much as I miss him, I do not view his persona through rose-colored glasses. My "good boy" was not perfect. Everyone, even Grizzly, has a flaw or two. Grizzly was a digger. He dug up our yard into heaps and chunks of dirt in his quest to find a phantom ground squirrel or gopher. On rare occasions, he found the prize he so arduously sought.

Grizzly's favorite task was his quest to get beneath our temporary house. We are living in a mobile home while my husband builds our modest castle. I have had a constant battle with Grizzly and his digging. He would tunnel and I would fill holes with boulders and logs or fencing, always to my failing. With all that hard work, Grizzly never made it under the house. He was too big. His smaller brother barked and cheered him on while Grizzly pursued the dream of the under-side. When the hole was large enough, his brother Fred would squirm into the mysterious world below our home. This was exciting for both of them. Fred explored and Grizzly pushed his nose beneath the foundation and smelled all the possibilities.

A few days before Grizzly had passed, he moved boulders and dirt and logs and was rewarded with not one, but two dogs

79

beneath the house because of his incredible efforts. The second dog is our petite foster failure Hedlee. We heard bangs and booms and ruckus like you would not believe. Of course, I had to go "rescue" Miss Hedlee, only to find that she was not frightened but joyful of the newly discovered underworld of the house, coming out with her prize, a live rabbit secured firmly in her mouth. To Grizzly, this was a dream come true. They all jumped and barked and there was tail wagging all around. Truly, this is a dog's version of giving a high five after winning the big game.

Not long after Grizzly died, I blocked off his favorite digging spot one last time. None of our other dogs had that drive to dig beneath the house. The "problem" that had plagued me for years had stopped. Believe me. I would rather have my boy back and the problem of that exploratory digging more than anything. In fact, I secretly pined for it.

Two days after Grizzly passed, I heard a noise outside. It was Fred cheering on Grizzly, only Grizzly was not there to be cheered on. I ran outside to find that Grizzly's dream continued. Dirt was flying everywhere as Fred cheered and barked and jumped about…only he cheered for another. Fred barked and Hedlee, not Grizzly, continued to dig more furiously. Now, for all his remaining days, Fred will not be alone in that mysterious underworld. His companion is and will always be a failed foster dog named Hedlee, and a big orange-and-white Brittany with angel wings.

THIRTY-NINE
THE MUTT

By the age of twelve, I became acutely aware of my mismatched body parts. Often, biracial children are born with such desirable physical characteristics that one might wonder, hey, how about a few more nationalities in that melting pot called the human body? My physicality is the epitome of self-service ice cream toppings gone awry. Yes, vanilla ice cream and sprinkles are good, but too many toppings and you could have one high-calorie mess; you could have... me.

God gave me broad shoulders and very big bones from my Norwegian great grandmother, whom I never met. At twelve, I was not yet tall but was unfortunately cursed with size ten, wide Flintstone feet. I eventually blossomed into a 5-foot-10-inch woman, but gained the squatty, well-rounded peasant body of my Lithuanian grandmother. God spared me my father's Russian nose and blessed me with his wavy, eastern European hair. My eyes are clearly Germanic, deeply inset chocolate brown with a hint of khaki green dancing about the iris.

Like many young girls, I longed to look like the popular cheerleaders at school who seemed to have all the advantages early in life. Gorgeous, naturally blonde Farah Faucett hair, clear, sun-kissed faces, a pearl-drops toothpaste smile and a football player on the arm. In contrast, I was the plain, studious girl of the library group, who watched "The Love Boat" each Saturday night, as my existence was devoid of teenage male attention.

Often, cheerleaders are like the pedigrees of the human race. They are the poodles, bichon frises and silky terriers. They are easily categorized and highly recognizable. My incongruous body parts are divided unequally into Russian, Lithuanian, Norwegian, German, Prussian and God only knows what else. I am, like most, the human mutt, the German Shepherd with the wiener-dog body. Oh sure, the poodle is exceptionally pretty, but there are thousands of pedigrees. The mismatched parts of this mutt are unique. It is a guarantee in life that you will come across many pedigrees, but it is a rare few that have had the opportunity to witness the illusive pooch known as the German Shepherd wiener dog. The uncommon prospect will most certainly bring delight, amusement and a memorable smile to all who have crossed her path. Woof!

FORTY

HAPPY NEW YEAR

Last night, after a wonderful dinner at Jack's Place, we went home, played with the dogs and then tucked in for the night. Jay was sleeping by ten o'clock, and so were the dogs. I finished reading a great book by Carlos Ruiz Zafon called "Marina." I shut down the Kindle and tried to sleep, but couldn't. I started to cry and woke up my snoring husband. He rubbed my back and said, "It's OK. I know." I was crying because I miss our dog boy. I stifled my tears with odd squeaks and snorts as Jay fell quickly back to sleep. Soon, he was snoring loud and bold. Usually, I turn on the fan to drown out his snoring, but this time, I did not. I listened to the rhythm and reflected on our good fortune. I am lucky to have him next to me. This could have been the year he left me for the other side, but here he is, snoring away. We are blessed by the modern miracle of medicine. As he fell into deeper sleep, the snoring disappeared and his breathing evened out.

I reflected on our day out with Annie. We take her running every other day. When she runs, she is attached to a harness and a bar, which is attached to our all-terrain vehicle. She loves to run. She jumps around and barks until we get moving, and then she takes off. It is a steady, controlled run along one of the

Edison roads in the Mojave Desert. The road is perfect because it has a few steep hills and valleys, a straightaway, rocky areas and a length of road I call the Sand Trap. The soil turns to sand and it is a particularly difficult area to run. I like this road for training, as it helps Annie gain her strength as she reclaims her field-dog figure. She runs about thirty minutes before heading back to the truck. Yesterday was particularly gorgeous outside. The sky was sunny and storm clouds were rolling in over the Tehachapi Mountains. We ran towards the storm clouds before heading back. It started to sprinkle. When we stopped, I wrapped Annie up in a towel, picked her up and put her in the back seat of the truck. She curled up in a ball, satisfied with her outing, and fell fast asleep.

A year of life is kind of like Annie's run. Most of the time there will be straightaways. There will be the occasional steep hill that is difficult to climb, and a few rocky roads. We may even get caught in the dreaded sand trap. Over time, we can build our strength and become tough like a field dog, ready to conquer whatever life brings us, whether it is the loss of a life like a beloved dog, or rejoicing after my husband survives a nearly fatal incident. Every little thing becomes even more important after such an event. In the end, even with our bumpy roads, we have survived another year and we are ready to make the 365-day earthly journey around the sun once again. We are glad to make this run again, as long as we have all of you.

FORTY-ONE
THE RAT

Training a dog for the field is important and has applications for home life. I can tell you now, Annie's training with her teacher, Paul Doiron, saved me yesterday.

My world-famous fear of things that walk vertically on walls came into play yesterday, when I discovered Annie with a big, fat, dead rat in her mouth. It was only the second time in twenty years I have seen one on our acreage. Wouldn't you know it? Each time there was a RAT, it was in Annie's mouth.

I went to the dog yard in the late afternoon to take Annie inside. Time for dinner, bones and belly rubs. There she was, with a big black rat with a snake-like tail on it, held softly within her gentle mouth. What is one of the first things a bird dog learns? "Whoa!"

Annie wanted to bring me that rat to hand. I yelled, "Whoa!" She stopped with the rat still in her mouth. "Drop the rat, Annie." She dropped the rat. "Come here, Annie!" She dropped her head down to pick up the rat, so she could bring it to me because I told her to "come." "Drop the rat, Annie." She dropped the rat again. "Come here, Annie!" She came, sans rat. Whew! And no, I did not barf in my mouth, but almost.

And the ravens had a fabulous dinner. Nice work by Annie's field trainer, Paul Doiron...and to Annie for remembering her commands.

FORTY-TWO
STARTING OVER

It has been nearly a year since Grizzly crossed the bridge. I think of him every day. I often see my husband kneeling over his grave, pulling out the weeds with tears in his eyes. I had not thought about the weeds until I saw him tending to Grizzly's resting place. Now I too go out and pull the tiny sprouts. It is one way to honor him, because he was such a good boy.

I can't tell you how much it meant to us to have the support of friends and strangers during the first few months after he died. But as the days rolled into weeks and the weeks turned to months, most forgot about what had happened, or at least the importance of the loss had lessened. But for us, it feels like it happened yesterday. We don't know how to completely let go of the pain.

Before we knew Grizzly had pancreatic cancer, we had planned on breeding him with our beautiful Brittany dog Annie, when she was of age and after she had become a field champion. But when we saw how Annie ran with her wide range and full field talents, we knew Grizzly was not her match. Annie received her Field Champion title two days before Grizzly succumbed to cancer. Honestly, when we found out his diagnosis; we decided he would never be a father. If the cancer were caused by heredity, it would be unfair to impose that risk on anyone. There will be only one Grizzly.

As of the date of this writing, Annie is pregnant. Her puppies are due nearly one year to the day that Grizzly left us. It was a difficult job choosing her mate. Of course, we wanted another field dog, one that was similar in size, with good structure and a similar gait to Annie's. But the way we went about picking her "husband" was not what a normal breeder would do. We did not rank the prospects by height, color, structure, shape of the head or any other physicality that most would consider important. We merely concentrated on the top field dogs. Then we went to field trials and met each dog. Were they nice? Were they quirky? Did they have anxiety? Was the dog fearful or aggressive? Did the dog spin in circles for no reason? Was the dog loving?

After all our research and scouting, we kept going back to the same dog. He does not look like Grizzly at all. This boy is mostly white with spots; Grizzly was mostly orange. We visited this field dog with and without his family. He is intelligent, kind and friendly. Then there is that something that I can't put my finger on, but it is familiar, and my husband saw it too. He turned to me and said, "He is the one. He acts just like Grizzly." We picked Annie's mate based mostly on personality and temperament. We know we can never duplicate our good boy, but we know what kind of boy we like, and we really like Sonny (Spanish Corral's Sundance Kid).

In less than two weeks, Annie will have her puppies. She will be a great mother. She will clean them, fuss over them and feed them while they grow big and strong. Then there will be the choosing ceremony. My husband will sit on the floor with the small puppy pile. One puppy will pull on his shoelace while an angel dog pushes the right one a little closer to my husband. Jay will pick up that puppy. He will turn his head and say, "I want this one," just like he did so many years before. He will pick a boy. His name will be Bear. Bear will learn to be a field dog. Jay will buy a horse and learn to handle his own dog and finally open his heart to love once again.

In two years, Jay and Bear will be at the starting line of a field trial, Jay on his horse and Bear by his side. Jay will blow a whistle and say, "Hunt-em up, Bear!" Bear will run. The rest of the world will disappear. He will run with the wind in his fur and the sun on his back. He will run with joy, with freedom and with a sense of purpose. He will be strong, bold and handsome.

And following behind Bear will be Jay, his horse and a big, orange-and-white dog with angel wings, ready to teach Bear to be a good boy.

FORTY-THREE

MY NAME IS ANNIE

My name is Annie. I believe in destiny. My father's father's father was a field dog; and so was my mother's mother's mother. I come from a long line of Hall of Fame field champions. This has and will always be my path. Even though I am a puppy, I have a destiny. My name is Annie. I am a field dog.

My name is Annie. I like to point and I run fast. I am like the wind as I cross over hills and valleys. I can smell fur or feather long before it is seen. Even though I am a teenager, if there is a bird, I stop and I point. I was born this way. It is called instinct. I stop, I point and I wait for my handler. My name is Annie. I am a field dog.

My name is Annie. Today I went to a hunt test to check my skills in the field. A lady walked by with her friend. "Look, there is a puppy!" The other lady laughs and says, "Oh, that is Annie. She is just a field dog." I smile, because that is what I am. But my Mom does not smile. Her eyes are wet and I don't know why. But when I am awarded with four orange ribbons in one weekend, my Mom smiled big and hugged me. My name is Annie. I am a field dog.

My name is Annie. I am at my first field trial. I am entered in a puppy stake. I am six months old. I wait and I wait for my turn. My Dad secures a special collar on my neck. It lets him know where I am at all the times. The men saddle up and the whistle blows. My Dad says, "Hunt'em up, Annie!" I run over hills and valleys. I smell and then find a bird in the bush and I point. My Dad flushes the bird and I stand strong. I am released to run again. The judges whisper and write on a paper. We return to camp and we wait again. They call the names of other dogs. White, yellow and red ribbons followed by applause. I feel tension in the air as I wait. Then I hear my name. My color is blue. My name is Annie. I am a field dog.

My name is Annie. My Dad says I am too good for him. But I know he is good and I don't understand. He sends me to a professional team so that I can learn to be a great field dog. The teachers keep me for months. I travel and compete throughout the Western United States. My parents visit me and are handed different colored ribbons during each visit. They bring me presents and hug me. When they leave, they cry. My name is Annie. I am a field dog.

My name is Annie. I like to compete. Sometimes I win and sometimes I lose, but what matters most is how I run, the decisions I make, the things I smell and the ground I cover. I don't care about ribbons. I care about finding a bird and the freedom of it all. I am doing what I was born to do. As I run, I collect points. I need ten to earn a field champion title. I hear my teacher call my Mom. He says, "Annie had nine points, right?" She says, "Yes." My teacher says, "Congratulations, she now has eleven." They are all proud and I get a treat. My name is Annie. I am a field champion.

My name is Annie. I am no longer living part-time with my teachers. I am home with my family and they are joyful to have me home. They take me on trips and runs and we have lots of fun. Then they take me to meet the dog that will be my husband. I smell him; he smells me. He is an Amateur National Field Champion. That means he is a dog of greatness. His name is Sonny. We become best friends for three days and then he leaves. My name is Annie. I am a field dog.

My name is Annie. I am hungry all the time. I eat as much as I want whenever I want. I take vitamins and visit my Doctor ever couple weeks. My belly is getting big and I don't know why. After two months, my belly swells and I have trouble sleeping. Then it happens. I am wet and I clean myself. At the break of dawn, I suddenly realize a dog can have more than one destiny. I am a field dog, but this is so much more important than that. I feel an enormous sense of responsibility and love as I look down and see what I have beyond the field. I am the creator of life. My name is Annie. I am a mother.

FORTY-FOUR
GRACE

A litter of puppies. Once grown, a dog can change the life of just one person. It is true. I have changed and grown and evolved because of each dog I have had in my life. I have learned about love, compassion, empathy and grace.

I was so careful when I planned Annie's first litter of puppies. I suppose I can be accused of being a secret control freak. I spoke to my friend about Annie's litter and she said, "Just don't do what So-and-So did. She went way overboard and ended up with one puppy in the entire litter." I thought about how I admired So-and-So. She is precise, educated and thoughtful. I want to be just like So-and-So.

The first thing I did was go shopping. Before birth, the puppies would have everything and anything they might possibly need. My husband watched as I studied different whelping kits. There was the standard model, the deluxe model, the super-deluxe model and the over-the-top, veterinarian-grade kit. Of course, I ordered the highest quality, veterinarian-grade kit. Then I purchased more things to supplement the kit. My husband looked in disbelief as the packages starting arriving. There was a special room heater, a heated whelping nest, multiple smartphone- integrated baby monitors, a headlamp, medical blankets, a stethoscope and a digital puppy scale. Each puppy even had a receiving blanket. My husband built the whelping box, ensuring it was the best. I scrubbed the whelping room until my fingers were raw. I purchased hospital-grade anti-bacterial spray for visitors to use. Everything was perfect, except life is not perfect, is it?

According to the skull count from the x-ray taken before the puppies were born, we were going to have five puppies. That is a small litter, but I was happy because it is a manageable litter for a first-time breeder. On the eve of day number sixty-three of her pregnancy, Annie stayed up all night. She was pacing and uncomfortable. I stayed up all night with her, petting and reassuring her until the break of dawn. By the time she was ready to give birth, I fell asleep. It was close to seven in the morning when the first puppy arrived, but I missed it. When I woke up, the second puppy had been born and the first one had been tossed aside. Annie had rejected the puppy and bitten off the rear legs and tail. A necropsy would later reveal the puppy had problems, but at that moment, the puppy was still alive and screaming. I called my friend Janice. Her husband is our veterinarian. She said, "Annie rejected that puppy for a reason. Now listen to me carefully. Don't hold this against Annie. She is an animal. You know what you must do. I will call Dave and he will meet you at the office." I wrapped the puppy up in a towel and drove straight there, worried about one and forgetting there were more on the way. Disheveled, disoriented and distraught, I ran inside Dave's office with the puppy. Dave picked up the pup, "It is a rough way to start your life, little girl." A girl. A beautiful girl. I cried. Dave said, "I will take care of her. I am so sorry." I said, "I know." At that moment, with tears in my eyes and pain in my heart, I said goodbye to the puppy. I named her Grace. Then Dave said, "You better get out of here."

I drove through red lights and raced back home as quickly as I could. Suddenly, getting there was beyond urgent as I did not know what might happen to the other puppies. I felt stupid. I was stupid. I left Annie alone. That could be a fatal mistake and it is my fault. I did not know what to expect. I ran inside, straight to the whelping room. There was Annie, as loving and content as any new mom could be, cleaning and nursing her babies. I looked down and started to count the puppies. I prayed, "Please God, let there be four puppies." I thought I was wrong. I knelt and got close to Annie and her new family. One, two, three, four...five puppies? That can't be right. Shaking, I put on my glasses and counted again. Five. Five beautiful puppies. Four boys and one girl. I cried out of joy and sorrow. I cried for what was and for what might have been. I cried about the cruelty of nature and the beauty and fragility of life. Most of all, I cried for the loss of Grace. There but for the grace of God go I; and there to God goes Grace.

FORTY-FIVE

WOULD YOU DO IT AGAIN?

On Sunday, Jay and I were discussing Grizzly, our Brittany who succumbed to pancreatic cancer seventeen months ago. We talked about his greatness and how much we missed him. Although it has been more than a year, I assure you, we are still grieving. Through my tears, I asked Jay, "Would you do it again? If you had a "do over," a chance to have Grizzly in your life as a puppy one more time, with all the joy plus a risk that you could lose him to cancer, would you do it again?" Jay thought about it for a split second and he said, "I already am."

The truth is, when we take in a puppy as our own we don't know what will happen. When they are born, they may live to be little old dog men and women, or they could die young because of an accident or disease. Fred and Grizzly are from the same litter. Grizzly is gone but Fred lives on. He will be ten this year, and he still dances a jig. As I write this, I consider the puppies that are sleeping right here in the room with me. They are beautiful, smart and joyful. We don't know what will happen, but because our hearts are open, we have fallen in love all over again. Without risk, there is no reward.

Would you do it again?

"I already am."

FORTY-SIX

BRITTANY UNION

Have you worked long hours without compensation? Stayed up all night guarding the humans from ghosts and extra-terrestrials? Barked out warnings that were completely disregarded? And worse, been scolded for doing so? Dug up the family lawn and kept it free of squirrels, rabbits and possums? Have you hunted hour upon hour without so much as one cookie? How many hours a day have you worked? Did you know that you are entitled to three cookies per hour with paid lunch? We are the Good Canine Citizen Brittany Union and we are here to unite all Brittanys in the fight against unfair labor practices. Did you know five missed cookie wages equals one—that's right, one—quarter-pound cheeseburger? It's true! How many burgers do the hu-moms and dads owe you? If you feel you have worked tireless hours without adequate compensation, we are here for you! We will immediately dispatch the Brittany Protective Services (B.P.S.) to investigate your claim. Protect your rights! Protect your freedom! Protect your cookies! Stand up for your BURGERS!!! BARK! BARK! BARK!

We have the experience you need to get the cookies YOU deserve.

This is a real paid Brittany spokes-dog. Finder's fees do apply.

Sincerely, Fred Benoit
All Around Good Canine Citizen

Working hard for you since 7 a.m. this morning when I came up with this cool idea.

FORTY-SEVEN

RED AND BLUE

There is always a story behind a story. Most know of our choosing ceremony, when Grizzly chose Jay and Jay chose Grizzly. The connection was instantaneous. That is how love works when it is love at first sight. But before there was a choosing ceremony, there was a contact made with a woman in Washington who had a beautiful litter of puppies. If I paid the gas money, she would drive all the puppies near where we live, to Quartz Hill, because that is where her mom lived. I had already picked a puppy and named him. He had pretty spots all over his back and a heart on his head. But that is not the puppy that came home with us. His name was and has always been Fred. As we were taking home Grizzly, Jay told the woman if no one wanted Fred, he would take him, too. Two days later, Fred and Grizzly were back together and today, Fred, our senior dog, is our eternal puppy.

Fred and Grizzly were like night and day. Fred liked to be groomed and dressed in sweaters. Grizzly was the hunter and was far more serious than his counterpart. The boys were very different but very much bonded to each other. They gave us joy each and every day. Fred still does.

When Annie's puppies were a couple days old, I photographed them with my Nikon. When I was processing the picture of the puppy with the blue collar, I studied his markings. I knew that he was not just "Blue." I knew deep down he was going to be "the one." I could not say anything to my husband because the puppy was his choice. I did show him the picture. Blue has a unique orange pattern that looks like he has angel wings on his back and a praying dog on his side. How many more signs do we need to know that this puppy was predestined to be ours? But the markings were not the most important thing; he needed a connection. Jay has held this Blue boy and played with him, too. But before any of that, it was love at first sight. Blue has always been the puppy who would be ours forever.

So, what about the puppy we call Big Red? Many are interested in both puppies and someone asked which one we had chosen because he was interested in Big Red. Which one? Blue or Red? At the time, I did not know. The official decision only happened as of yesterday. Jay decided the only way Big Red would leave us is if he went to a field-trial home. Yes, the person who wanted Red runs his dogs in field trials and that was the first test. He already had committed to taking home our female puppy. He contacted the airline to see if he could switch his tickets around and get an animal transport for them instead. This particular airline does not transport animals. He could take a puppy up front if the puppy could fit in a carrier under his seat, but they don't transport dogs alone. We don't either. We won't let our puppies go into the cargo hold of an aircraft, but he did not know that at the time. He decided to take only one puppy, and that puppy is still the female now named Nosey. She will be flying to Illinois, up front, with her dad, which left the fate of Big Red undecided.

I have been playing, cleaning and fussing over all the puppies. One puppy has been fully engaged with me. He will climb over everyone, run by his Mom to greet me and has done this each day for the last week. That puppy is Big Red. He wants to be held, and he likes me to tickle his belly. He is big and dominant, and it is a toss-up between Blue and Red as to which will be the leader. We want a strong dog who is a good decision maker and is out in front in the field. Blue or Red? Red or Blue? Red needs to be in the field, too. The last time we chose a puppy, my husband picked just one. A few days later, there were two. Today I am happy to say the same thing has happened. Jay chose Blue and then we chose Red. The answer to the question is upon us. Which puppy? History has repeated itself and now there are two. Welcome to the pack, Leona Valley's Blue Puppy and Red Puppy! You will both be good boys.

FORTY-EIGHT
THE BEST LAID PLANS

"The best laid plans of mice and men often go awry."

If I would identify personality characteristics for myself and my husband, I would say I am more of the creative free spirit and he is a thoughtful realist, a meat-and-potatoes kind of guy. I dream, and no matter how much I plan, sometimes things just don't turn out how I imagined.

I planned on having a Western theme for all our future Brittany dogs. After all, Annie is "Annie Get Your Gun". When I considered Western names for the boy we planned for our pack, Billy the Kid sounded just right. A couple of months ago, my husband agreed. But once you meet a puppy, things change. Jay told me he did not like the name "Billy" for the pup. Truth be known, the name "Billy" did not suit the puppy we identified as "Blue." We called him "Blue" because that was the color of the collar placed on him the day he was born. But really, we can't just keep calling him "Blue."

The night before last, we sat in the puppy room with Annie. Jay and I picked up and hugged each puppy. Jay hugged all the puppies except for Blue. I picked up Blue, handed him to Jay and he held him close. Then Blue put his head on Jay's chest and smelled him like he was the best thing to smell on this earth. I had tears in my eyes because the same thing happened nearly ten years ago, with Grizzly. I said, "I know Billy is not the name for him. But I do know the right name, the one that suits him best." Jay looked up at me with tears in his eyes when I told him the new name. He said he would think about it and he did. We did not discuss it again until that night. We were in with the puppies again, holding and playing with all of them. Then Jay called Blue the new name. I said, "Is that his name?" He said, "Yes." The name that suits this little guy so well is in honor our good boy Grizzly. What do you call a puppy marked by angel wings and a praying Brittany? He will now and forever be known as "Bear."

FORTY-NINE
HOW DO WE KNOW?

How do we know if there is a God? The puppy does not know. He sleeps there with his belly up, lifting to and fro. He dreams of places far away, of bunnies on the hill; he kicks his legs as if he runs, while a hare sits very still. I was with this puppy on his first day, the beauty of life anew, knowing that the days of puppy are oh, so very few. One day the puppy will be a dog. Oh, the joy we will have shared; and as his days continue, he will always know I cared. For in the time between life and death are days filled with love. It is clear to me that this puppy was sent from that place that is up above.

How do we know if there is a God? The puppy does not know. He is a piece of heaven on this earth; the seeds of love he sows. In my days from beginning to end and all the in between, the days I have spent with this puppy are the best I have ever seen.

FIFTY
ADVICE TO THE PUPPIES

Dear Puppies,

I have some human wisdom that I would like to share with all of you:

Nosey: When you hardily dig and successfully remove the litter from the cat litter box, it is no longer a cat litter box. It is just a box with a bunch of sand and crap that has been randomly flung everywhere.

Big Red: Crying and jumping around will not result in me picking you up...even when you throw yourself down and kick your feet in the air as part of your bitter protest.

Rusty: It is not nice to tackle your brothers. Remember, you are small and big boy Rowdy will sit on you.

Rowdy: Sitting on your brothers is not a way to make friends. And no, they don't care if you are incredibly cute.

Bear: I was so proud of you and your siblings when you started to use the puppy pads as your potty destination of choice. Therefore, I am terribly saddened to find that you have decided to play tug of war with Red, using every puppy pee-pee pad placed in your domain. Shredding it to pieces is a nice touch.

However, it is economically infeasible to rip up pee-pee pads, as these are disposable items and must be replenished frequently. It is financially wise to play tug of war with your TOYS rather than pee pads. Using actual toys is cleaner, is better for the environment and not so gross.

Love, Me

FIFTY-ONE

PUPPIES

We puppies are up at the break of dawn with a quick little pee and a tiny little yawn. Mommy feeds us; then we all start to play; what a great way to start our new day. The shadows of the land lift by high noon; give us a moment and we will sleep very soon. When we wake up again it is time for us to eat. Come here Mommy, give us our treat! Then we pee and we poo and we say, "How do you do?" Time to tackle; time to play; it is time for the puppies to have it their way. But then we slow down, so tired are we; we turn into a puppy pile, that's what we be. Now it is late afternoon and we all want to eat. Come here, Mommy, please give us our treat! She comes once again and cleans up our bums; then she feeds us our meal beneath the setting March sun. Tired and happy we fall fast asleep. In a few hours, we will be ready to repeat.

FIFTY-TWO
WILL YOU LOVE ME?

Will you still love me when I am no longer small? When I grow big and strong and just a little tall?

Yes Red, we will love you when you are a grown boy, we love you more and more each day.

Will you love me if I am not a champion? If I don't win a blue ribbon? Or if I make a mistake?

Yes Red. We will love you no matter what. If you win, we will celebrate. Remember, blue is just a color. It is you that we love.

Will you still love me if my face turns white? If my whiskers turn gray and my legs become weak?

Yes Red. We will love you more than the day we knew you would be ours, and with each day that goes by, we will love you even more.

Will you love me when I am gone? Will you remember who I am? Will I be in your heart and dreams? Will I be yours when I am a star in the sky?

Yes Red. We love you today as our little puppy; tomorrow as our grown dog; we will love you even if you make mistakes. We will love you when you are old and gray. We will love you after we take our very last breath. Even when you are naughty, you are our angel on earth. We will love you today, tomorrow and the day after forever.

FIFTY-THREE

THE FIELD TRIAL

Someone asked me to describe a field trial. Of course, you could read the "American Kennel Club Field Trial Rules and Standard Procedure for Pointing Breeds"; but that does not describe the feel, the scene or the true depth of the activity.

I woke up at 5:30 this morning. The Lance camper is holding three sleeping dogs and a snoring husband. I look outside and see the stars are up high as others start their generators and coffee makers to prepare for the Fall Field Trial at the Spanish Ranch. Horses are fed, and dogs are prepared, as the camp stirs with activity.

The first brace is at 7:30 and our teenage dogs, Moose and Kody, are competing in the Open Puppy stake. It is their first time at a field trial. The memory of last night's dinner is still fresh in my mind. Joe said, "It is not about winning, losing or even ribbons. We are here to find the very best dog for today. It is about taking care of and preserving this land. It is about honoring the dogs."

During a field trial, dogs compete two at a time until all the dogs have had their turn. Each dog is judged for their bird finding ability, their ground application, decision making skills, innate desire and their ability to honor their brace-mate. With two dogs per brace, one dog wears a yellow collar, the other orange, so that each is identifiable by the judges. For this event, Moose wears a yellow collar because she is the bottom, or second dog named in the brace. The top dog is always orange. There are typically two judges on horseback; and each dog has a handler, who is usually on a horse as well, but may opt to walk instead of ride. Each handler may have a scout to help locate a dog, but a scout may not interfere in handling the dog.

For this field trial, my husband Jay sits on Smokey, his twelve-year-old Tennessee Walking Horse. This horse is new to Jay. Jay is nearly sixty years old, is a beginning rider and his horse has a bit of an attitude. We stay silent and do not tell anyone that the horse reared up and stepped on his foot an hour earlier, breaking two of his toes. They already know Jay's life has been hanging in the balance. I hand Moose's leash to Joe. "Can you release her at the line?" He smiles, "Sure." A whistle blows as the dogs disappear into a deep narrow canyon filled with wild coveys of quail waiting to be discovered. This is where it all happens, brace after brace. The dogs do what they were born to do. Not one bird is shot. They are found. The handler flushes the bird while the dog and its human companion wait while the bird flies away. They mutually hope to find another bird once again.

There is something uniquely beautiful about a field trial. This is a true example of the symbiotic relationship between human, dog and horse, all working together as part of a tacit partnership that has been divinely formed over thousands of years. At a field trial, this forgotten bond is restored and flourishes. At the end of the day, it is the eyes and minds of the well-experienced judges that determine which dog earned the blue ribbon that day, in the pursuit of the dog earning points to become a field champion. But a field trial is so much more than ribbons and points earned towards a championship title.

My husband has recently had serious struggles with his health. He almost died, not once, but twice in the last year. He has a bad knee replacement, bulging disks in his back and a heart that wants to up and quit. This man, who at one time was 2/10th of a second short of competing as a swimmer in the Olympics, still has that innate desire to compete, even though his body says he can't. At the Spanish Ranch field trial, multiple people helped him get on and off his horse. Someone else offered to scout for him. One small but mighty person wrangled Jay's horse when the horse was misbehaving. Another seasoned expert gave him pointers on horsemanship. When Jay's dog was on point, Jay got off the horse and flushed the bird while his dog Red held steady. It was the people at this field trial who helped my husband get back up on that horse and finish the brace.

During dinner that night, the winning dogs were announced. Because we have an excellent dog trainer and because of the intervention of many truly kind people, our dog Red came home with a third-place ribbon in the Amateur Gun Dog stake. It is Red's and Jay's first time placing as and with, an adult dog. A third-place ribbon does not earn Red a single point towards his championship title, but the memory of that village of field trial people who literally picked up my husband, will never be forgotten.

When I walked with Jay back to our camper that night, I heard Roy Rogers singing "Oh give me land lots of land beneath starry skies above, don't fence me in." I looked up at the canopy of stars blanketing the beautiful Spanish Ranch and I smiled. Jay held Red's yellow ribbon in one hand, my hand in his other. "You know I don't have much time left." I said nothing and squeezed his hand a little tighter because I know he is right. Our time together is now shorter than it is long, but we still have some years remaining. With the time he does have left, Jay has decided what he really wants, and it involves dogs, horses, salt of the earth people and the wide-open countryside.

I imagine heaven for Jay is something like a field trial at the Spanish Ranch. The land is wide open, gently rolling with cattle, an expansive bridge and an abundance of wildlife. The trial grounds lead to a narrow canyon covered with native oak trees, scrub and coveys of wild quail. In the depth of the canyon are horses, dogs and great friends while Roy Roger's sings, "Send me off forever but I ask you please, don't fence me in."

What is a field trial? It is not a rule book. It is the land. It is the sky. It is wide open spaces. It is kindness and true friendship. It is the symbiotic relationship between human, dog and horse, all working together as part of a tacit partnership that has been divinely formed over thousands of years. It is here at a field trial where this bond is not just nurtured, it flourishes.

FIFTY-FOUR

THE BRITTANY CLOWNS

I have had Brittany dogs for almost a quarter of a century. Each one has brought love and adventure into my life. The first set were from a rescue. They were inbred and sweet. I call them my warm-up Brittany dogs. One was blind from birth and the sisters took care of each other. Never a bit of trouble, ever. The years have gone by and each dog has wiggled its tail into my heart and my mind. Brittanys are known as the clowns of the sporting dogs, and sometimes I wonder why I do it again and again and again.

This morning I woke up, or someone woke me up. My eyes are like slits. It is still dark outside. I look over at the cat. She is in her bed on the nightstand and she is looking down at my bed in disgust. I could be imagining her "look," but I am not. My bedspread is missing. I look over at Bear's bed and he has the bedspread, all of it, and the edging has been pulled off by some unknown assailant. I sit up and look on my bed. Kleenex. Kleenex everywhere. I am covered in Kleenex. I look at the nightstand again. The box of tissue is missing. I turn my head and see Red throwing the empty box up in the air gleefully. I shout, "Noooooo!" But it is too late. I jump up and take the empty Kleenex box and start grabbing tissues that are torn up, everywhere. Some pieces are too small and I will need to vacuum. I look over at Bear. Something is wadded up in his mouth. I pry it open and find Kleenex. More and more Kleenex. OK boys, it is time to go outside.

I leash them up along with the other dogs. Our dog kennel area is about 100 feet from the house. Our entire property is not fenced, so I must leash them up and take them there. OK, they take me there. It is playtime. The white stuff on the ground is not snow, but a thin coat of very slippery ice. I start to slide as they pull me. I think I am going to fall. I pull them back and take them inside the house to wait for the thaw. That cat is horrified by their reappearance. Her can of Fancy Feast must wait.

Last night, Bear had a bad case of the zoomies. It happens every night, but last night he was particularly obnoxious. I caught him standing on the dining room table, without the aid of a chair to get him up there, and he pulled off the fake flowers I had wrapped around the chandelier. OK, yes, they are old and probably should come down. I yell, "Nooooo!" But it is too late. Bear jumps down and he is running with flowers in his mouth. He passes a bunch over to his brother, Red. Now they are both running with fake flowers. I grab Bear, his eyes are dancing with glee. He bites off a petal, smiles and then swallows. Why don't I ever learn? Why!!!??? I grab the remaining flowers and throw them away.

The teenage Britts are now nine months old. The breed is not for the faint of heart. It takes a long time for them to become "good" dogs. My boys know how to turn on lights, open cabinets and slide open the mirrored wardrobe doors and take what they think should belong to them. A couple of weeks ago, Bear was in my naughty pretty-things drawer. At least I think it was him. He pulled out every naughty thing he could find along with stretched stringy things that were meant for only my husband. I caught Bear with a wadded up something in his mouth and a piece of it was in between his teeth like dental floss. Yes, it was some stringy and delightfully fun panties.

Today the boys are inside because of the ice outside. I give everyone a marrow bone so that I can hop in the shower. It is good and hot and I enjoy the bathroom while it steams up. The cat sits on the counter, still waiting for her Fancy Feast. Red comes in and sticks his head behind the shower curtain to see what I am doing, and then he disappears. The shower is super-hot. It feels great. I turn off the shower, reach for my towel. It is missing. The cat has a smirk on her face and slaps her tail around. Where is my towel? I pull out a new towel and reach for my bra and panties. Where are my bra and panties? No. Nooooo! The morning zoomies have begun as I listen to what sounds like two teenage Brittany dogs laughing and carrying on while their Mom is dripping wet and wondering why she wanted another Brittany clown in her life... or two.

As it turns out, I have had selective memory all my life. Each puppy has done "something" and all have done a little of everything. From drinking my coffee, to emptying out the litter box or ripping up the mail. Each dog has their own tale to tell. And before they take their final breaths I will have the most amazing memories, not just of the bad, but of the good. The kisses, the hunts, the dancing and the joy. Every year I have and will always have stories about these splendid orange-and-white canines known as the sporting-dog clowns. And nothing gives me greater joy and more frustration than chasing a dog flying through the air with a bra dangling freely from his mouth. And in the end, I will always call him my good boy.

FIFTY-FIVE

RED'S UNBELIEVABLE BELIEVABLE STORY

I had a bad accident and I don't know what to do. It was early in the morning, so early the sun had not woken up yet. Dad left for work and my human Mom was still sleeping. I wanted to be right next to her so I jumped on the bed and put my head on the Dad pillow. If felt really good. Then I started to suck the end of the pillow. Then I bit it. It is a neat pillow with shreds of memory foam inside. All the sudden, the memory foam started to pour out of the pillowcase. I got nervous. The only way to cover up the memory foam spilling out was to eat it. I started to eat all the memory foam while human Mom slept. Then I threw it up all over the bed. Even more stuff came out of the pillow. When human Mom woke up, she had memory foam confetti all over her body. My DNA is on the bedspread because I barfed. I acted like nothing was wrong and I don't think she is on to me, at all, but I need a story of what "really" happened because I don't want to get in trouble.

Here is what REALLY happened according to Red Benoit, all-around good dog boy. I was sleeping in my crate when an entity came into the room. It was evil and its breath was foul, like a rotten fish. The temperature dropped considerably and I shook in fear. Fear for myself, fear for my family and fear for the pillow that was sitting on the bed helplessly. Ghost? I think so. Suddenly, the ghost swoops down and grabs the pillow and shakes it violently. I am so distraught. I don't know what to do! The extreme fear has caused me to lose my bark. Suddenly, and with malice in its heart, the ghost starts to empty the filling from the pillow and tosses it carelessly all over the bed! Oh, my GOD! Help me! The ghost spots me and knows that I AM A WITNESS!!! The beast turns its attention to me. ME!!! It is going to shut me up and keep me from barking out what has happened. It starts to viciously shove memory foam pieces down my throat. I gag and cough. Then I play dead, which worked, because the ghost left. That is when I barfed on the bed. That's my story and I am sticking to it.

I am not a hero. I am merely a regular Brittany dog with a story...just like you.

FIFTY-SIX

I GREW UP POOR

I grew up poor. It was the kind of poor that blended into the scenery and went unnoticed. At the time, there were no programs to save me from my environment. The beauty of having nothing is there are no expectations. I did not expect anything so when something wonderful happened, it was a big deal. Most of all, it just felt good.

With extreme poverty, choices were a part of survival. Should I get a prom dress or have breakfast for the week? I did not go to the prom or any other dance when I was in high school. Survival was my first priority. When the volleyball couch asked me to try out for the team, I did not. I could not afford to buy a uniform. How could I? When he asked again I turned away, embarrassed by my circumstance. No, it was not meant for me. I was not sad about these choices. It was my lot in life and I had no expectations. Anything better is just frosting on a cake.

I have Brittany dogs. Chosen for their utility as a hunting dog as well as being good companions, I never thought about the beauty of the breed. I did not pick out pretty dogs. Our decisions on dogs have mostly involved which lines were best in the field, were smart, covered the most ground, and had the best overall utility. I did not have "pretty" and I certainly did not seek "pretty." Pretty has never been part of my life.

When our field champion, Annie, had her first litter, we were very excited. The sire is an AKC Amateur National Field Champion, and both parents come from a long line of Hall of Fame Brittanys. We kept two puppies from the litter. Early on, I began to prepare them for their life as field dogs. This involved conditioning them for loud noises, activities, children, anything that could potentially frighten a dog. When my friends asked me to go to show handling class so the boys could learn to be with other dogs, I thought it was a good idea. The class was held at a very busy park filled with children, joggers, tennis players, ducks, a big fountain, swings and so much commotion that of course Red and Bear would benefit just by being there. They loved the activity and enjoyed the class, particularly since they ate hot dogs as an incentive to be good and stand pretty during class. My field dogs were learning the art of show, even though their background was virtually void of any show dogs. Truth be told, their mom is slightly out of size for the breed. Some snickered and called her Amazon Annie, and I knew it.

When a puppy reaches six months of age, it is eligible to compete in show. My field puppies could compete. I reverted to my irrational, high-school self. Surely my dogs could not compete. They are brilliant, athletic future field dogs. I don't have anything pretty. How could my field dogs just come to a dog show and compete? I worried about them being on display; being sized up, literally, as field dogs are typically tall. Would they be accepted? Could they fit in? Would someone know that we don't belong? My friends encouraged me to enter the boys, and so I did.

I hired a professional show-dog handler and worked with the boys to "stand pretty." My dear friend helped with them during the week and on the weekends so that they were groomed to look the part. Truth be known, by the time they were old enough to go to the show, they looked beautiful. I never had pretty or beautiful, but there they were, two really good-looking boys.

I drove to the show grounds in the San Fernando Valley, at Valley College. The parking attendant did not care that I didn't really belong there. I was a girl from Jersey Street, but honestly, I could have been from Rodeo Drive and no one would have noticed. Everyone was busy putting on the finishing touches on their dogs. I took my field dogs—OK, they dragged me over to their handler. She smiled and offered me a Twinkie for breakfast. Yes, a Twinkie. I liked her right off the bat. I did my best to keep the boys out of the dirt and off the asphalt. Then, all of a sudden, we were all running. We were late to the ring. We were running with the pups and other dogs to the sporting-dog ring. Just on time.

It happened so fast. Red was up first. He was entered in the six-to nine-month-old puppy class. He was the only one in his class and he won. No surprise there. Then it was Bear's turn as American Bred. Next to his handler, he looked beautiful as he glided around the ring. Another ribbon. Then the dogs were matched up with each other. All around the ring; round and round they go…and stop…stand pretty. Red and Bear each cocked their head, stood tall and looked the part. Then another ribbon. There must be a mistake, but there wasn't. Bear's handler was given a ribbon. He was the Winner's Dog. My Bear.

I could say it is a mistake and give back the ribbon. A poor girl from Jersey Street doesn't have pretty things. No dresses, dances or sparkles. She certainly could never have anything nice enough. I could say it is shallow of me to consider the beauty and structure of a dog as important. But it is the package that is important. Smart, strong, capable, built well and looks beautiful. I will never have a prom or be on the volleyball team. I made choices in my life that were geared towards survival. But for just one unremarkable moment in the middle of the San Fernando Valley, I had something in my life that stood pretty and looked beautiful. The best part is, no one even noticed.

FIFTY-SEVEN
BREXIT

Before Bear leaves this small town to learn how to be a big field dog, we have had several discussions to prepare him for his journey. Yesterday, we discussed the geopolitical and economic consequences of Brexit and the potential change in the world order. He seemed to be enthusiastic about our discussion as I put his leash on him to take him to the dog yard. He began pounding the door with his front paws and jumping up and down all about Brexit.

Me: Bear, how do you feel about Brexit?

Bear: I think it is a good idea. Bear should be able to exit any time he wants.

Me: What?

Bear: I need to pee. Let me outside.

Me: Do you know what Britain is?

Bear: No. Br-exit means Bear gets to exit any time he wants. Now let's Brexit!!!

And that is the world according to Bear.

FIFTY-EIGHT
TWLIGHT RUN

Sometime before twilight, we took the dogs running in a low valley surrounded by mountains on three sides. The valley is bisected by a dry ravine filled with rabbit brush. Buddy the greyhound shepherd remained on a leash by my side. Fred ran up and down the ravine looking for Jack, the rabbit.

Hedlee, Red and Bear headed towards the mountains and ran up and down the sides. The air was frigid. The dogs loved the cold air and kept running. One dog became the leader and ran straight up the face of the mountain and at one point was nearly vertical and seemed to touch the sky. I cringed. The dog continued up and down the mountain face. The others followed but not quite as high.

Which dog had the strength and drive to go vertical? The dog that at one time was held in kennel so small that when she came to us her back legs would not fully straighten. The dog that never ran until she was an adult. The dog who was afraid of everyone, especially men, is now free to embrace life as it was meant to be. It took twenty-nine months for her to become her true self, which includes running vertical and touching the winter sky.

Amazing. Just amazing. She is Magnolia's Hedlee Lamarr's *Happily Ever After*. And we call her Aunt Hedlee.

FIFTY-NINE
GRIZZLY AND BEAR

Last night Jay and I talked about how much we miss Grizzly. He has been gone almost two years. Shortly after he died, I mean within a day, I had many people recommend that we get another dog. We already have a lot of dogs and a new dog can't replace the old one. I know people want to help, but I always thought it was odd when someone said, "Get another dog."

Jay has often joked If he outlived me he would bring his new girlfriend to my funeral. It is a threat because he never wants to be a widow and he knows I am insanely jealous. We also know that if I outlive him, I would be devastated to go on without him just as he would be lost without me. If Jay were a widow, he would mourn and cry and endure. He would not bring a new lady to my funeral. But I do not expect him to grieve forever. I want him to be happy. Would Jay's friends and family advise him to "get another wife" at my funeral? That would be wildly cruel if not crazy. There is only one Jay and there is only one of me...or at least I think so. I understand this is an extreme example, but it is how I feel. If I lost a friend to cancer, I couldn't just run out and get a new one. I am certainly not going to go husband shopping should my beloved suddenly pass. And we did not "get a new dog" because we lost Grizzly.

We have had Brittany dogs for a quarter of a century and we have had exactly one litter. That does not make us "breeders" nor do we want to be breeders. But with respect to what had happened to Grizzly, we wanted complete control over our next dog member of the family. We wanted to raise the puppy from birth. Meet him from his first breath and love him until his last. Annie had her litter of puppies almost a year to the day that Grizzly died. The choice of puppy was obvious for Jay. He was attracted to the temperament that was most like his best last dog. But this puppy would be different. We have learned so much with every dog we ever had and just that knowledge meant the puppy would not be the same as any other. Before Jay chose the puppy, the puppy chose him. You all know that puppy as Bear.

Last night, Jay lamented that Bear is not like Grizzly. Yes, there are strong similarities. They look similar. Mahogany orange saddle, block head, square build and equally strong. If Grizz were still alive, Bear would look like his younger sibling. Then there are the Grizzly-isms. He liked to hug, particularly before bedtime. He had an Elvis smile. He was always fussy before bedtime and had trouble getting comfortable before finally falling asleep. Bear hugs too. Not exactly like Grizzly. He presses himself to the chest, but Grizzly took in the smell as well as pushed himself tightly for a hug. Bear is equally fussy before bedtime and has trouble settling down. He has an Elvis smile too. Both dogs had/have a stoicism, particularly with an injury. Both have been Buddy's best friend. That's where the similarities end.

Jay had tears in his eyes when he discussed Grizzly versus Bear because Bear is not Grizzly. He loves Bear, just like he loves his brother Red, only different. But could his love for either dog be as deep? They are not the same dogs. The love for each will always be different. It is human nature to compare. We all know, no one can live up to the memory of an angel dog, not even a good dog like Bear. Or can he?

I typically go to sleep a half hour after Jay. All the dogs come in, eat a cookie and go to bed. The routine is the same every night.

Each dog has their sleeping spot. I enjoy watching Bear as he prepares himself for bed. The first thing he does is he climbs up on Jay. He sits on Jay like he is a chair. He turns one way, then the other. He huffs and puffs and is fussy. Finally, he will lay down flat as a pancake on top of my husband. I don't know how, but my husband usually sleeps through these activities. Bear then reaches for Jay's face and gently washes it. Eventually, Bear will place his big head on Jay's back, or shoulder or leg and fall asleep. Bear is devoted to his man like no other dog, except Grizzly.

How will my husband know that Bear is his second "once in a lifetime" dog? Time. Everything takes time. There will be a day when Jay will wake up to Bear's loving routine as he finds dog spit thoroughly covering his face. He will not find it repulsive, even if it is a bit yucky. Bear will hug him and Jay, as he always does, will hug him back. He will not think of another dog at that moment, even though he has loved like that before. Bear, with his devotion, is ready to be Jay's best dog; and Jay is a lucky man to have more than one best dog in his lifetime. He just doesn't know it yet, but he will.

SIXTY
TIME FOR A NEW HAT

If you have read my Facebook profile you would know, "I like dogs; I like cats; I like people who wear funny hats."

I like funny hats. I have a collection of oddball winter hats that I wear when I take the dogs running. My favorite has a raccoon face on it with fake braids. It is embarrassing, it is fun and it makes me smile.

It snowed early Monday morning. It was just a dusting, and by late afternoon there was little evidence of the white stuff, except a light blanket covering the hilltops of the Angeles National Forest. It was bitter cold and windy out when it was time to take the dogs for their run. I bundled up thoroughly. Cobalt blue long underwear, thick jeans, boot socks, scarf and of course a funny hat to cover my ears. I chose a hat with a pseudo Nordic print with two strings of fist size pom-pom balls, dangling from below each ear. The strings could be tied to secure the hat better, in case of large wind gusts. Perfect. Jay looks at my attire and says, "Not a wise choice for a hat. You are asking for it." I looked at him quizzically and wonder what is wrong with my hat?

Getting the dogs ready for a run is quite an experience. Hedlee, Bear and Red wear GPS. collars because they are big running dogs. Fred, a senior citizen, does not. Buddy is injured and rarely wears one. I go in the dog yard carrying the three collars. Mayhem ensues. Fred jumps on me because he wants to wear a collar even though he does not need one. Buddy jumps on me because he thinks I am going to leave him behind. Hedlee runs circles in the yard and avoids the collar. After running in circles a few times, I take hold of her gently. She shrinks down to the ground. She thinks it is a shock collar. We assume the hoarder she was rescued from must have used one on her often. I put on Hedlee's collar and she recovers from the ordeal. That leaves Bear and Red.

Red likes to push everyone out of the way. "Move over everyone, it is my turn." He pushes Fred and Buddy and starts walking on two legs, batting his front legs at me rapidly. I hold his front legs, kiss his face and then handily put on his collar. One dog to go.

Jay starts backing up the box Scion to the dog yard and things get even crazier. Bear's turn. Bear has developed a new routine. First, he likes to rearrange the dog furniture. We have the giant dog igloos. They are heavy-duty. Doesn't matter. He grabs the door frame in his teeth and starts moving a house, and then another. They are arranged in a circle. He drags them around until they are organized just perfect. He jumps on top of one house; to another and another. He likes to jump on each house and when he is ready, he launches himself through the air and jumps on me. He assumes I will catch him. The first few times he did this, I did not. I did not know I was supposed to catch a flying 50-pound, over-sized Brittany. He trained me. Now if he flies, I catch.

Bear danced upon each house and steadied himself before the launch. He has a giant smile on his face. Then he starts to fly. His legs stretch, muscles tighten as his mouth opens wide. Wait, his mouth opens wide? He is jumping to my left side and will not land in my arms. It happens in slow motion. He flies, he grabs the highest pom-pom ball on my hat, pulls and lands on the far side of me, with a string of balls in his mouth. He starts running. Red sees the balls and he starts running too. I scream, "Hey, you took my balls!" I am running, too. My funny hat now sits lopsided on my head and is torn. We all run together. Then Red and Bear play tug-of-war with the string of pom-pom balls. The string breaks, right down the center. Two balls for Bear; two for Red. I take hold of Red and pull the balls out of his mouth and throw them over the chain-link fence. I miss. The balls land inside the dog yard. Red picks them up and starts running again and we all run in circles. I am yelling at the boys. As you well know, they are laughing. I finally get a hold of both boys and take away the pom-poms. I put Bear's G.P.S. collar on his neck, open the double doors to the dog gate and they all jump into the Scion. Jay looks at me and says, "What took you so long? And I told you that was a bad choice for a hat."

And yes, they do go running every other day. I should have known better. Time to buy a new hat.

SIXTY-ONE

OUCH

The Brittany dogs wake up at 5 a.m. each day. They don't know if it is Monday or Saturday. They never sleep in and don't know about the laziness of a weekend morning. I take them out to their kennel close to sunrise. If I can, I will try to go back to sleep.

Old man Buddy stays inside. He appreciates sleep. Annie, Red, Hedlee and Fred go outside. Because our kennel is far from the house, and because our acreage is not fully fenced, they are leashed up. I take them slowly. All the dogs are leash trained and are good on a leash, except if there is a random distraction. I am careful to walk slowly to make sure that the dogs are lined up, and pulling is not tolerated.

They are doing an excellent job this morning. I am particularly impressed with Red. The leash is slack and he walks by my side. I continuously tell him he is a "good boy." To enter the kennel, we walk through two doors of a building and then through a gate. It is safer for the dogs.

When we are within a foot of the building, everything is suddenly haywire. It happens so fast. Suddenly, my entire body slams against the building. My arm stretches sideways and hits hard with a thud. Rabbit. Field dogs and rabbits. Too much pressure and nature kicks in. They ignore all the leash rules. My hand feels wet as I pull them back. I use all my strength. With their efforts and ardent protests, the rabbit got away. I drag all four, now wild field dogs, into the building. Is it raining? No. I feel all wet. Dripping. I rub the fingers of my left hand together and feel the dampness on my skin. I unleash the dogs and put them in their kennel.

No time to give them their breakfast. My hand is filling up with liquid. Blood. I throw down the leashes, close the building and hurry back to the house. I cup my hand. It is irrational but I do. I cup my hand to prevent the blood from covering the earth. Why does it matter? It doesn't. I don't think the earth cares if it carries my DNA. By the time, I am inside the door of the house, I start to hyperventilate. I wake up Jay. At this point I am crying. He thinks one of the dogs has escaped and then he sees my hand. It has been ripped by a nail in the shed building. "Oh God," is all he says. He rushes me to the kitchen. The blood pours into the sink as he washes my wound. He cleans my hand with alcohol and finally, direct pressure allows the blood to coagulate. He bandages me up and as soon as he knows I am fine, Jay goes back to sleep.

Buddy watches the chaos. He knows something is wrong. Buddy the greyhound shepherd, who hates to be accidentally touched while he sleeps, does not climb into his own bed, but jumps upon ours. Mind you, he has severe nerve damage and jumps on the bed with just three legs. He looks at my hand. He stares at me. Then he does something he normally does not do. Buddy, the Keeper of the Brittanys, sleeps next to his mistress and makes sure she is safe. Eventually, sleep claims me as the fall sunrise slices patterns through our wood window blinds. I do not stir until the sun is up and high.

Even in pain, I know I am blessed. I am blessed to have a husband who will bandage me up while thoroughly exhausted and a dog who will watch over me because he is a good boy. As for me, the gash and bruises will heal just fine. And my husband is installing a cable system to take the dogs out, stretching from here to there. This won't happen again.

SIXTY-TWO
BEAR'S NEW TOY

Oh, yes, he did. I was working in my office when Bear ran in with his brother right on his tail. Looks like Bear has a toy and Red wants it. Wait a minute. Bear ripped up all his toys. He has none. My phobia? Falling on rocks. Heights. Rats. Oh...and dead things.

I realize it is a dead thing. Could be a squirrel. Could be a rat. I start to run away from Bear, who is proudly carrying the dead thing. Red chases Bear. Bear sees me run and chases me with the dead thing. Jay gets ahold of Bear while I hide and shriek. Jay says, "Bear...Release!" Do you think Bear wants to give Jay the dead varmint he found while digging in the yard? No.

It was pulled out of Bear's mouth. No bite marks. No spit. Not officially identified and no, I don't want to know.

SIXTY-THREE
THE FIELD DOG

He stands at the end of a bulky red lead and waits for the whistle to blow. His entire body quivers with the expectation that beyond the frost-covered hill will be a covey of wild quail.

His Human releases the lead as a shrill sound fills the early morning air. Within seconds, Red reaches a low sandy knoll in this inhospitable land known as the Mojave Desert. His nose ingests every scent with such intensity that there is no doubt as to where he must travel. He instinctively pivots towards the cloud-covered January sun, flies over fields of rabbit brush and creosote. Suddenly, as if hitting a brick wall, Red slams to a stop. His right front leg lifts slightly and his tail stands at twelve o'clock as his body stiffens. He leans forward as his entire being is filled with excitement. He won't move an inch until his Human has arrived. He has found his quarry.

He is a field dog.

SIXTY-FOUR
SMILEY MILEY

Smiley Miley has spent the day at our house while her dog-mom, Nancy, is at work. She will be leaving us soon, but now has a list of demands.

1. Miley is a "princess" and has not been treated as such. She believes her name does not sound royal enough. She says from now on we must call her Milealani. It sounds more exotic.

2. She has discovered that she likes to have bottled Sparkletts water like all the dogs here enjoy. Therefore, Sparkletts must be ordered, pronto. She likes it served cold.

3. Today she was served an organic soup bone, cut to her size, special from the butcher at Whole Foods Market. Yes, Whole Foods is expensive, but as a princess, she deserves the very best.

4. She now listens to classical music and expects it to be played each time she enters the room. She is partial to Mozart.

5. With respect to organic food, she noticed the dogs here enjoy homemade stews and have scrambled eggs made

from cage-free eggs (also from Whole Foods). She would like to have an omelet for breakfast, made fresh and served with her special water.

6. She should be supplied with plenty of gophers in hidden holes throughout your property with permission to dig deep and get dirty. The dirt on her nose must remain, as it is her new style.

Her royal princess says thank you, and remember to curtsy each time you present yourself to her when entering and exiting the room. Of course, don't you dare look at her directly in the eyes.

SIXTY-FIVE

CONFESSIONS OF THE BRITTANY DOGS

We Brittanys were pleased when Pope Francis declared that dogs do go to heaven, but are concerned that maybe we can't get through the Pearly Gates. We don't know about religion or faith, but we decided we should do what Catholics do and confess our transgressions, just to be on the safe side.

We, the Brittany dogs of Leona Valley, are sorry we may have caused undue harm to our human companions. In order to be good dogs, when we make mistakes, just like humans, we learn from them. We promise to try harder next time, except for Fred, who says he already knows everything there is to know. The following is a list of wrong-doings, some of which may be attributed to Red, Bear, Hedlee, Annie and Fred. We know that Annie has been gone at field-dog school, but we are blaming her for some of this stuff anyway.

1.   Ate the hand stitched appliqué off Mom's expensive wool sweater (Annie)

2.   Cleaned out the litter box and ate the Roca (Bear, Hedlee and Fred)

3.   Pee'd like a boy (Miss Hedlee)

4. Took the cat's bed and blanket (Bear)
5. And ripped it up (Bear and Red)
6. Cleaned out the naughty pretty things drawer (Bear)
7. ...and stole panties and used them as dental floss (Bear)
8. ...and played tug of war with said panties (Red and Bear)
9. "Found" a bra and hid it (Red)
10. Took Roca and placed it under the decorative carpet (Hedlee)
11. Woke everyone up at 3 a.m. and encouraged all dogs to evacuate to steal hidden treats (Fred, multiple times)
12. Danced on the dining room table (Bear)
13. Jumped on top of the kitchen counter (Annie, Bear and Red)
14. Stole fake flowers and ripped them up (We were doing you a favor: Red and Bear)
15. Turned off the toilet valve (Bear)
16. ...and ate it (Bear)
17. Unrolled the toilet paper (Red and Bear)
18. Ate napkins (Bear)
19. Emptied the Kleenex box (Red)
20. Ate Kleenex (Bear)
21. Ate the house (Red and Bear)
22. Dug a hole, or two (Bear, Red, Annie, Fred, Hedlee)
23. Brought a dead animal in the house (Annie, Hedlee, Red, Bear)
24. Bit the wall and took off the molding (Bear, Fred)
25. Stole human food (Red, Bear, Annie, Hedlee and Fred)
26. Disconnected the electronics in the car (Annie)
27. Ate a seatbelt (Red and Bear)
28. Gave Mom a black eye (Red)
29. Gave Dad a fat lip (Red)
30. Took out some of the carpeting (Bear)

There may be other things that we have done. We are busy dogs and it is hard to keep track of our hectic canine schedules. We feel this list is a fair representation of the acts of "no-no-bad dog" stuff we have committed. But as you know, it is easy to dwell on the bad (especially with such a long list) and forget about the good. But the blessing of having a Brittany as a member of the family is that your memory will become short and your heart will become full. Despite all our shenanigans, we truly love you. This is why we are with you now, and it is exactly why you will find us on the other side, regardless of what the Pope declares.

All good dogs go to heaven… including naughty good dogs like us.

SIXTY-SIX

THEY KNOW

When I started writing the dog essays, I promised myself I would write about everything and anything. Nothing is off limits, including my own "stuff," the secrets that are buried for no one to see or know. My husband doesn't know; my friends nor my siblings. No one knows what happened. How could I say it without falling apart into a million pieces? I can't say it. But I can write it.

I have thought long and hard about my relationship with all dogs. When did it begin? How did it happen? Is there a reason why any dog and every dog instantly becomes my friend? Dogs are intuitive. They can read intent and instantaneously know your heart. My relationship with dogs is gloriously beautiful, painful and something that can't be described in a few sentences. Dogs know and feel the echo of my past, and the anguish that I have carried for many decades.

When I was eight, my father brought home a beautiful, I mean stunning, Gordon Setter. His name was Dundee. I don't know how Father could afford such a majestic creature. We had few toys and many times went without things that are considered necessities. I don't know if someone got rid of Dundee, but here he was in our house and he was ours. I loved him instantly.

I lived in an era in which children should be seen and not heard, and my father reminded us of this often. If we were even slightly out of step, or minutes late from school, the belt came out. It was Dundee who watched and worried. One day, Dundee could not take it anymore. He was bred as a hunting dog, but he was our friend and protector. My father was yelling about something and Dundee went wild, jumped up, slashed Dad's face with his teeth and then knocked out his lower front tooth. I remember the blood running down my father's chin and the anger in his eyes. He left with Dundee and Dundee never came back. We didn't even get to say goodbye. My father never said what happened to that dog, but us kids knew him and knew the truth. That was the day Dundee died. As a child, I thought Dundee's death was my fault. It wasn't, but that is what I thought at the time. If I was better, quieter and even more invisible, Dundee would have lived.

I never told anyone what happened with my mom. How could I? Who would have believed an eleven-year-old girl? No one. At the time, I did not realize my mother suffered from mental illness. I did not know she was diagnosed as a paranoid schizophrenic with psychotic tendencies, but I lived it. I don't think anyone can imagine what it is like to live with something as horrible as mental illness, until you are in the middle of its chaos. What bothered me most is that my mother did bad things in front of me and acted normal, or so I thought, around other people.

At the beginning of each school year, I received one new pair of shoes. In fifth grade, I had a growth spurt. I grew so much that, by spring, my shoes no longer fit. My toes poked out the end. One day, the shoes were so tattered they fell off my feet. I was sent home from school and could not return until I had a new pair. My parents lived from paycheck to paycheck. There was no money for new shoes in the budget. I remember when Mom picked me up from school, she was mad. She drove fast and mean down Tampa Avenue, heading south towards the Northridge Mall. That is when I saw a puppy in the middle of the road. "Mom, stop! There is a puppy in the middle of the road!" Of course, I wanted to save the puppy. That is a normal response. She didn't stop for the puppy. No. Her car veered to the left, in the direction of the puppy, and she purposely ran over it. A thump, and then I heard a blood-curdling scream. It seemed like it was someone else screaming, but it wasn't. It was me. Terror. I felt terror and sadness all at the same time. She kept going and drove faster, like she was some sort of demon. She didn't care. I asked her, "Why...why...why!" She said, "I was doing it a favor." I can't explain how truly nightmarish she was in the way she said it. Honestly, I thought I was going to be next. When we got home, she did not remember killing the puppy, but I did. That scene haunted my dreams for many years. It still does.

Dogs know. They can hear the echoes of my screams and taste the salt from my tears. They feel my regret and my eternal sorrow. They know from the depths of my soul, I love them all. Dogs know. They know it all. The good, the bad and the insane. And for whatever reason, they have more than accepted a broken person like me. Because they know my heart. They know all of it...and it is still OK.

We each have our own cross to bear. This one is mine. I don't carry it alone. Each dog has helped me carry it, and they always will.

SIXTY-SEVEN
Wrong Side of the Bed

Have you ever had a day when you really woke up on the wrong side of the bed? Yes, I did today. I took the dogs out at 4:30 this morning. That is their normal time to get up, go potty and, hopefully, go back to bed for an hour or two. By the time Red came inside, he was amped up and ready to play. I climbed back into bed, ignoring his exuberance, until his tongue landed in my ear. My ear! Then he scooted himself under the bed like an army man. Thump. Thump. Thump. I yelled, "Red!" The thumping continues. Then, Hedlee joins in the army game. The two culprits are leashed up and taken outside. It is 5 a.m. When we reach the kennel, I unleash the wild dogs, feed them and clean up whatever "stuff" they left me the day before. It is almost sunrise when I drag myself into the house and back to bed. Sunlight slices through the window blinds as I wish I had my sleeping mask, but someone (Yes, Red) pulled it off my face yesterday and ripped it up. It is now 6 a.m. I put the pillow over my head and hope to sleep another half hour.

I wake up late. I need to hit the road. I run around like...well, like Red, getting ready as quickly as possible. I need to do field work for four jobs today in completely different areas of Los Angeles. How on earth will I get all of this done? I might not. I am in and out of the shower in a flash. Brush my teeth. My electric toothbrush dies. I forgot to plug it in. I blow dry my hair. No time to curl my bangs. I flip my hair upside down and generously use my Bed Head hairspray. Smells...different. It is not hairspray. It is Right Guard. I sprayed men's deodorant on my hair. Not good. Too late now. Gotta go.

I drive south on Bouquet Canyon Road. Halfway down the canyon I realize I forgot to put eye drops in my eyes. My eyes are dry and when this happens, I produce so many tears it looks like I have cried a river. I know my makeup is smeared, my mascara gone. My eyes are completely irritated. I reach in my purse and feel for eye drops. Bingo. Found my eye drops. I will put them in my eyes when I stop for gas in Santa Clarita. When I stop, I grab the eye drops knowing that I will have instant relief. Squirt. Not eye drops. Ear drops from the earache I had two months ago. My right eye is now burning. I feel the puffiness beneath my eyes. Now my nose is running. Ugh. No Kleenex in the car. Paper towels. I blow my nose on a paper towel and wipe off the remainder of my makeup.

Traffic was unusually light. I made it to the city quickly and was in downtown Los Angeles; then off to Hollywood. I need to pee but no time. I finish my work in Hollywood and head north, to North Hollywood. I spot a fast-food burger restaurant. I don't like this place, but they have restrooms and I need to pee. I park my car, run inside and go straight to the bathroom. Whew. Wash my hands. I feel dirty. I wash my hands and my face. No paper towels. The blower thing, and that is no way to dry a face. I leave with my wet face and a drink.

Next stop, Lake Balboa, which is really Van Nuys but let's call it Lake Balboa because it sounds better. Almost done, then I can head north. My next stop? The market. I am going to pick up something for dinner. I decide to go to the pretty market that has specialty things. I am always happy when I go to the pretty market. I pick up some dog bones, honeydew melon, deli items and hand cream because I ran out. The clerk is sharp. The hand cream I grabbed was the sample. Of course. When I walk outside with my bags, I try to open a car like mine. Well, really, it is only similar in color. Eventually, I find my car and head north. Thirty more minutes until I am home.

When I walk through the door, Jay has taken a box with something big apart and he is building something. He is fiercely hungry and I feed him quickly. Red and Hedlee are outside, waiting for me. When I get them, they are both covered in mud. It was muddy pool-party day. I bring them both inside and each dog gets a quick bath. Finally, I sit down on the Lazy Boy and who is in my lap? Red. He smiles. His eyes say it all. He waited all day to see me and now his day is complete. With Red in my arms, I realize all the "stuff" I did and messed up today was not important at all. It felt like a bad day. I was completely out of sync and off kilter. At the end of the day, it did not matter. At this moment, I am in a quiet house with a dog in my arms as the sun sets in the west. Tomorrow is a new day. I will not spray Right Guard in my hair or put ear-ache drops in my eyes. I won't wash my face and hope for a paper towel or wonder if it is OK to stick my head in the hand dryer. I am not buying new hand cream. It is almost the weekend. The one thing I will do tomorrow is I will hold Red again, just like I did tonight. Only tomorrow, I will smile and remember some days are better than others, and sometimes, there is nothing better than a dog in my arms as the sun is setting on a beautiful summer night.

It is easy to remember all the bad things that went wrong in a day. If we choose to do so, it is also easy to forget.

SIXTY-EIGHT
DESTINY, PART I

Fate is defined as the universal or ultimate agency by which the order of things is presumably prescribed; that which is inevitably predetermined.

Is there a predetermined path by which a puppy's future will inevitably travel? What I am about to describe is Annie's second litter, if the puppies were ever to be born. I say this now knowing that two separate paths could have been taken.

Here is what happened with the second litter of Annie puppies and their unknowable fate. I relate this because Annie had serious reproductive issues following her first litter. She ran in the fall field-trial season the year after the birth of her puppies. But something went wrong. From winter to spring, she had continuous heat cycles. A female dog typically has two heat cycles per year. Annie drifted in and out of heat cycles from month to month. Her body was literally dumping eggs. This condition, if allowed to continue, would be detrimental to her health. There are two courses of action. She could be fixed, never to have a litter again. Or, we could put her on birth control and see if this would straighten her system out. We did not know if we wanted another litter. Her reproduction specialist recommended we try birth control and we followed her advice.

Annie was on birth control in the form of Cheque drops for several months. Her body had not completely returned to normal. She was overweight, even though she ran for several miles in the desert every other day. We put her on a strict diet and continued to prepare her for the next field season. We hoped she would be the spring field-trial surprise: slim, healthy and energetic, just like she was before. By mid-December, she was running a solid eight miles on her field runs and loved it. In fact, she was crazy about running and couldn't wait to go.

Her boys, Red and Bear, came home from field-dog school for winter break. They were home for six weeks. They did not join her on her runs.   She continued to strength train. In mid-December, the boys went back to their trainer. Annie didn't lose an ounce. In fact, she started to gain weight, a lot of weight.

In late January, I took Annie to her veterinarian. I was concerned about her continued weight gain even though she had a vigorous exercise program. Maybe it was a false pregnancy. Could she be pregnant? I couldn't see how that was possible. She wasn't in heat. She just got off the Cheque drops. Dr. Dave took a good look at Annie and examined her thoroughly. "Let me take an x-ray." In the meantime, my husband called me and I told him she might be pregnant. "She can't be pregnant. If she is pregnant, those puppies are inbred. You have to get rid of them." he said. "I can't do that. I can't!"

"Just ask Dave." he said.

Moments later, I was called into the back office to look at the x-ray. In Annie's belly were six perfectly formed, almost full-term puppies. "When did the boys leave? Looks like you are having a litter of puppies!" We took out a calendar and counted. The puppies were due in two weeks. Then I worried. In fact, I panicked. Annie was running her entire pregnancy. She had no pre-natal vitamins. I was concerned about her nutrition. Dave gave me good advice. He said, "Nature knows best. If there was something wrong with the pregnancy, it would have self-terminated. She is strong, healthy and she is from a good line. It is called line-breeding and it is not necessarily a bad thing. If you have a line of dogs with something bad, like a hereditary defect, you are doubling down on the bad. But if you have a line of excellent dogs, you are doubling down on the good. You have excellent dogs."

"My husband wants to terminate the pregnancy. He does not want line-bred dogs."

What happened to the litter of puppies? This was the first time in my marriage when a difference in moral opinion clashed and crashed quite hard. Get rid of the puppies? Keep the puppies? Now let's consider their fate, if the puppies lived and discovered their destinies.

What I did not know until today is the puppies were each given assignments that are part of their destiny. These things were whispered to them at birth, and it makes them happy knowing they will make a difference in many lives. What did I find out? Since they are puppies, with very short attention spans, they did not disclose complete details. They provided little snippets here and there. This is what I do know.

One boy puppy and one girl puppy will comfort the sick. They will help them forget their bad circumstance simply by being happy and loving. Making someone feel happy is contagious. The happiness they will provide will save someone's life. This is a reminder that they are doing God's work and will make their family very proud.

Two puppies will send their boy to college. They love their boy; will watch for him out the divided glass window, and will miss him when he is gone. These puppies will remind their own boy that the best things in life are often right beneath the roof at the place we all call home.

One puppy, when she turns old and gray, will be in a wedding. She will carry the ring when her human sister is a bride. Even though this puppy is beautiful, when her human sister walks down the aisle, all eyes will be on her and her parents will cry with joy.

One puppy will run through the high desert and will point at wild quail. He will make his dad proud when he brings that bird to hand, time and time again. His human mom will smile when she sees he has become the very best friend of his half-brother. They will be inseparable, forever.

One puppy will be so loved that on the day he dies he will be cremated and the ashes will be put in a small box, and when his human passes on, the box will be placed in his human's casket, so that they will be together for eternity. Only the family will know the truth and their hearts will smile.

But did we terminate the pregnancy? Would we? Did the puppies meet their destinies?

***

SIXTY-NINE
DESTINY, PART II

One week following our trip to Dr. Dave's office, I slept in the guest bedroom with Annie. I did so each night and on day number sixty-three at 7 a.m., the first puppy was born, followed by five more puppies. By 11 a.m., all the puppies were born and today are known as Dutch, Skye, Sadie, Banjo, Moose and Kody. I slept in the same room with them for their first six weeks of life. I did this to make certain they were safe, healthy and loved.

The truth is, my vet and dear friend would not terminate Annie's pregnancy. Nor could I let that happen. My husband and I decided it was fate that created six puppies and it was divine intervention that brought them into the lives of some very wonderful people. The puppies were meant to live and give love to a dad, a mom, a veteran, a boy, a girl, a college-bound son, a young doctor and others who are sick or broken hearted. In the grand scheme of things, does it really matter that a litter of six puppies in fact lived their happily ever after? Yes. It matters because each puppy became a member of a family. They are the smile at the end of a hard day. They provide comfort and joy and to some, a sense of purpose. The puppies are needed, wanted and loved by many. In the end, it not only matters that these puppies were born; they were divinely chosen to live.

SEVENTY

LESSONS

I have the belief that every person crosses our path for a reason. It could be for a moment, just a split second in time. It is fate that has made sure our paths have crossed. Those who are with us longer, are meant to teach us something.

The same holds true for dogs. For whatever reason, I have two more puppies in my life once again. I have no clue as to what lesson I am going to learn from these two souls, but there is a plan, and a shared path and one day I might know whatever "it" is supposed to be.

I have thought about the dogs I have in my life and in my heart. What have I learned from them? Each one is different and unexpected.

Grizzly is the dog who taught us how deep a love for a dog could be. He was and has always been our heart dog. We did not know it when we brought him home. But after gingerly caring for him until the day he succumbed to cancer, with the enormous grief that followed, nothing could ever compare. Grizzly taught us that a dog is not just a dog. A dog is the member of our family.

Buddy, our shepherd/greyhound mix, was our difficult dog. I say this only because he was obsessive compulsive. He paced day in and day out, and he barked up a storm. When he, too, was sick with cancer, this pack leader let me carry him up and down stairs. With Buddy, we first learned about patience. But we also learned that no matter how strong you are, it is OK to ask for help. He was and will always be remembered as the leader of the pack and the Keeper of the Brittanys.

I have learned many things from Annie. People often joke that girl dogs are called bitches for a reason. I would never refer to Annie in that manner. She is the sweetest, kindest dog I have ever met. I grew up without a mother to regularly take care of me. Annie showed me what it is like to be a good parent. She revealed the truth about motherhood. It is something that is good and wonderfully beautiful.

Fred was the dog that was not supposed to be ours, but here he is, sitting beneath my desk. He is the senior of the pack. Fred has taught me about acceptance. He has accepted every new member of the pack with open paws, and is particularly fond of the puppies. Fred taught me it is not necessary to be top dog. Sometimes it is just OK to be everyone's very best friend.

Red is the most joyful, over-the-top dog I know. He smiles at the world and the world smiles back. What I like about Red is his desire to make sure we know he loves us, by giving us a kiss each and every night. Red has taught me to make sure the people I care about know they are appreciated and loved.

Hedlee is the surprise of the group. Coming to us from a hoarding situation, she had zero socialization when she moved to Leona Valley. Honestly, I did not think she could ever get "better." Hedlee is proof that with time, gentle encouragement and love, one can conquer almost anything, for Hedlee has done just that. She is the most amazing thirty pounds of fluff I have ever met.

Bear was chosen from the litter because of his temperament. He is gentle and quiet, much like Grizzly. There is an underlying playful and mischievous quality about Bear. Bear was the dog who taught us the most valuable lesson of all. After one has loved and lost, it is OK to love again. In life, it is possible to have more than one heart dog. In fact, if you are truly blessed, you will have one, then another and another.

I don't know what lesson will come to us with the addition of our new puppies named Kody and Miss Moose. But I do know our hearts and minds are open and we are ready for whatever lessons come next.

SEVENTY-ONE
SADIFIED PUPPIES

We puppies believe we have been harmed by the humans that keep us here. We feel upsetedness. First, we see the big dogs running around without a containment around them. We think this is unfair and we would like to run free-range, with full access to the entire house and the yard. We were told we can't run around outside as we please because there is an owl and he will carry us away. Puppies don't fly! How can our friend the owl carry us away? We want outside anytime we want, and we don't give a hoot about the owl—or his friend the hawk, for that matter.

We have even been kept in jail while inside. We are deeply crybabily about this situation. Yes, crybabily is a word because we say so. We believe the jail time is because of discrimination. We know we have not been trained to pee and poo just outside, but that is because of the owl and flying away. Should this keep us confined to a small area with just a little bit of food, a thousand toys and water? We are so sadified, we climbed out of our pen and stole some shoes and hid them. We feel justified in doing so. The humans won't find the shoes because of their poor sense of smell. That is not our fault.

Is it considered blackmail if we tell them where the shoes are located, once they release us from prison?

Sincereterrifically yours,

Kody and Moose
Resident Puppies

SEVENTY-TWO
STURDY DOG POOL

Mom ordered us a GIANT DOG POOL from the AMAZON!!! Twelve inches deep, sixty inches round with PVC and heavy canvas construction. Mom read the reviews and everyone said the pool is sturdy and is made just for DOGS!!! Our new pool is REALLY expensive, but Mom figured it would last us all summer long.

It's FUN when we jump inside. We all fit in the pool together!!! Then Uncle Red says, "Let's taste this corner!" We do whatever our Uncle Red says because he is so smart. Soon, we are all chewing on the pool, but nothing happens. Then suddenly, one of the panels that held up the pool came out. Whoa! This is a great idea, Red!!! We start to dismantle the expensive pool. Then the water goes WHOOSH and it all comes out at the same time! We get super wet and continue our project of taking all the panels out of the framing of the very expensive DOG pool. When we are done, we spread all the panels all over the DOG yard, chew the corners off some, and put the canvas base in a tiny pile. We still don't see any PVC piping. It must be false advertising!!! And if our pool is from the AMAZON, shouldn't it come with parrots and big exotic plants or something? Since this pool is advertised as a sturdy DOG pool, shouldn't it last more than a few hours? Have other DOGS had this problem?

We think we have a case against the manufacturer for not sending a STURDY DOG POOL, plus a PARROT and big giant AMAZON LEAVES. We are sadified because we don't have a GIANT DOG POOL anymore.

Sincereterrifically yours, Kody & Moose (The Feral Beasts); and Red (The Terrorist)

SEVENTY-THREE

A DREAM COME TRUE

For almost twelve years, we have driven Buddy by Reitano Ranch. Each time we pass by, he barks vociferously, convinced that his bark will bring the cows closer. He is half greyhound, half German Shepherd. He wants to herd the cows but will also do what a sighthound will do: he will chase. He has never been close to a cow...until tonight. Tonight, while driving the dogs home from a run, two cows were out on Elizabeth Lake Road. Buddy knew well in advance of us that the cows were out and started to bark. We thought it was a normal bark bark bark—until we came upon two running cows. Jay pulled over, put on the emergency flashers and with another neighbor worked to wrangle the cows. One cow scooted under the fence, back to the ranch; one young cow ran up and down the street for a good forty minutes. At one point, Jay used the Scion to herd the cow—with Buddy in the car! Oh my. This was Buddy's dream come true. He has waited all his life to come this close to a cow. It ran next to the car, around the car, in front of the car; and then...eventually, onto the neighboring cattle ranch for temporary safe keeping.

Yes, Buddy, dreams do come true. Even for an old dog like you. If Buddy could talk, he would tell you it was worth the wait.

SEVENTY-FOUR
BUDDY, PART I

Our German Shepherd dog Ralph was the best dog we ever had. He guarded and took care of our two Brittany girls until they were laid to rest. Then he, too, took his final bow. He followed the girls to the rainbow bridge.

We wanted a dog like Ralph, another German Shepherd. When we arrived at the Lancaster Animal Shelter, we were overwhelmed. So many great dogs needed and wanted homes. I spotted a sweet girl and thought she was the one. She wasn't a pure shepherd, but she was really a nice girl. Jay wasn't interested in the girl. He was interested in the imperfect looking boy at the other end of the kennel. One ear up, one ear down and skinny. His legs didn't quite match his body. His fur was gray and black with a bit of tan. That is the dog we took home. He is a greyhound with a German Shepherd coat and ears. His name is Buddy.

Buddy waited six months for his first best friend. When we brought Grizzly home, Buddy thought that the puppy was just for him. They played for hours and hours. Buddy's life was full. He was thrilled. A few days later, another Brittany came to live with us, Grizzly's brother, Fred. Two Brittanys for one Buddy.

Nothing could be better, ever. It was his fate. That is when Buddy became the Keeper of the Brittanys.

Grizzly and Buddy were inseparable. Each night they sat together beneath the setting sun. After wrestling, Grizzly would jump up on the patio table and Buddy would sit nearby as they watched the wildlife wake up and run through the fields of our beautiful Leona Valley. Eventually, they would come in, but often, they wanted to stay out until late at night. They were closer than brothers. They were a team.

Buddy was triple blessed with the arrival of another Brittany, a puppy named Annie from the great state of Texas. He loved Annie like he loved the boys, but she required training and lessons that they never needed. He worked with her and made sure she was a strong member of the pack. That is when another Brittany arrived, a foster dog named Hedlee. She was scared and he knew it. He welcomed her with open paws because she needed a home. Buddy had four Brittany dogs to care for now and he did so because he loved it. He was and has always been the Keeper of the Brittanys.

Buddy knew when Grizzly was sick. I could see his concern. There was nothing any one of us could do. If he could trade places with Grizzly, he gladly would have, because he was and has always been The Keeper. When Grizzly died of cancer, there was only one dog that truly mourned, and that dog was not a Brittany. It was Buddy. Buddy stopped playing; in the middle of great sorrow, he lost his joy. He kept the remaining Brittanys safe, but that was all. His heart was broken. One night, while we were deep in slumber, Buddy howled the greatest, deepest howl. The sound was eerie, like it came out from the bottom of his soul. He howled for what he lost and for what would never be again. I hugged Buddy and I cried, for I knew that was his version of tears. The Keeper had lost one of his own. The Keeper had lost his Brittany.

After Annie became a field champion, she had a litter of five puppies. Buddy looked in on the puppies and watched them, but did not play with them. He kept them safe but he did not want to love like he had once before. Two puppies stayed to live their happily forever after with us. Buddy tolerated them but did not train them. That was Annie's job. He did, however, take his job as "The Keeper" seriously, for now he had five Brittanys who relied upon him. One night, he singled out one puppy. I know why he picked that puppy. It was the same reason we chose that puppy. Buddy played with that puppy each night, training him to be a leader. That puppy is named Bear. Bear was named after Grizzly because of his similar temperament. It had been nearly two years since Grizzly had passed when Buddy decided to play with Bear. It was awkward at first but then they roared and wrestled and ran. I was so happy when I saw Buddy play once again. What I did not realize was that Buddy was not really playing; he was training his replacement. He could not be the Keeper of the Brittanys forever. He knew he was sick. Buddy has cancer.

In April, it will be three years since Buddy played with Grizzly. Buddy has seen his last spring, his last summer and his last fall. As winter approaches, I wonder if he will see January. He might, he might not. I already told him it was OK to leave us if he wanted. We will not hold him back from his fate. He has served as the Keeper of the Brittanys and now it is his turn to be free. Free to play, free to run and free to be with his best friend once again. We will not keep the Keeper. He belongs on the other side of the rainbow, above the stars and beyond the moon, in a valley filled with wildlife and one big orange and white dog ready and willing to show him the way. They were meant to be together forever...and they will.

Not yet, but soon.

SEVENTY-FIVE
BUDDY, PART II

His life is not about the moment he took his last breath, although I can now say Buddy took his and is at peace. Life is a collection of moments in a totality of many years. He was a friend and a protector. He earned the title "Keeper of the Brittanys" and that will be his name for eternity. What happened after we said goodbye? I will try and tell you what happened, to the best of my ability.

We took Buddy to his vet, who is our dear friend of many years. Dr. Dave compassionately gave him two shots. It was the second one in which I saw the reflection of heaven in Buddy's eyes. He felt the blessing and went straight to the light.

Buddy traveled to an amazing bridge with shimmering prisms offering an array of colors lining his path. The bridge led him to a land much like our own, only better. Buddy met a man named Saint Francis, who welcomed him with open arms and showed him different places he could stay. Buddy saw there was a land for German Shepherd Dogs; he visited another place for sighthounds. Buddy worried because he was not one or the other, but both. He didn't think he would fit in either place. Saint Francis said in an encouraging voice, "Don't worry, Buddy, I have a special place waiting just for you." Suddenly, two regal looking dogs, Digby and Luke, stood on each side of Saint

Francis as he said, "These dogs will show you the way to the Land of Brittany." "There is a land called Brittany?" Buddy was surprised he could speak like a human. Things were different in this place.

Luke and Digby took Buddy over hills and into a valley of great beauty. The lush landscape gently rolled and was covered with wildlife. He saw a covey of quail, rabbits, squirrels and a large pond. Off to his right he noticed a modest home, much like his earthly home, except there were two patio tables on the deck, not one. Then he spotted him, his very best friend, sitting on top of a patio table. Grizzly smiled. He waited nearly three years for Buddy. Grizzly jumped down, wiggled his butt and readied to play with his old friend.

Buddy said, "Why am I here?" Grizzly threw his pal down and howled, "We are in the Land of Brittany!" "I know, but why am I here?" Grizzly said, "Look around." That is when Buddy saw them. Not one or two, he saw all of them. Thousands of Brittanys. Playing, pointing, swimming...everywhere. They were all here in the Land of Brittany. "But I am different. I am not a Brittany." Grizzly looked at his favorite friend in the eyes and said, "You are here because you are "The Keeper." You have protected and served Brittanys with great honor on earth and you have been chosen to remain "The Keeper," not just for our pack, but for all Brittany dogs."

Buddy knew this was the place where he belonged. He walked to the empty patio table. From far away, it looked like an ordinary table, but up close he found it was special. The glass sparkled like diamonds and etched in the side was his name:

BUDDY
KEEPER OF THE BRITTANYS

He jumped onto his glass table and Grizzly joined him as they watched over an enchanting faraway place. Somewhere above the stars, beyond the moon and over a rainbow bridge, is a land where all Brittanys go when they leave their humans behind. Some call it heaven, for that is what it truly is, but here we call it the Land of Brittany. And they lived in this land forever and happily ever after.

Buddy Benoit
February 1, 2005 – December 26, 2016

SEVENTY-SIX

THE LAST WORD

I saved this part for the very end, because it is the most important page of the book. The day 103 dogs were seized was the day their lives changed forever. Shortly after triage was complete, seven dogs were given the mercy of death. Four more were laid to rest in the immediate weeks that followed. Eleven lost souls. Each dog was given a name before they passed. A name means they mattered. A name means they had an identity. A name means at one moment in time, they were touched and loved by a human. I pray their second chance at a real life, beyond the rainbow bridge, is gloriously beautiful, for that is what they truly deserve.

I don't know if this book will be read by anyone beyond my circle of friends. But I do know the names of these lost dog souls must be written down for eternity to remember their hardship, remember their sorrow and remember their lives had meaning. To the Magnolia dogs who never had a chance to live in a forever home, we are truly sorry. You were all good dogs. You came into this world with nothing. You left this world with a name and a kiss.

Sarah, Jessee, Charlie, Trooper, Louise, Joey, Buddy, Hooker, Johnny, Shelby & Magick

At the end of the rainbow...there is a dog.

The End.

GLOSSARY OF DOGS IN THIS BOOK
REGISTERED WITH THE AMERICAN KENNEL CLUB

Annie: *Field Champion, Leona Valley's Annie Get Your Gun*

Banjo: *Banjodeep Michael Shah*

Bear: *Leona Valley's Sonny Bear*

Dutch: *Deputy Dutch's Paiute Warrior*

Fred: *Just Plain Fred, IV, Master Hunter*

Grizzly: *Grizzly Discoveries, Master Hunter*

Hedlee: *Magnolia's Hedlee Lamarr's Happily Ever After*

Kody: *Leona Valley's Kodiak Bear*

Miley: *Champion, International Champion, Crosscreek Millicent of the Mountains*

Moose: *Leona Valley's Micro Moose*

Nosey: *Dodge City's Big Nose Kate*

Puppy: *Sigrid Von Deutsche Hound*

Red: *Leona Valley's Sonny Red Side Up*

Rowdy: *Red River Rowdy*

Rusty: *Rusty Dan's Paiute Sentinel*

Sadie: *Sadie Rose of the Valley*

Skye: *Skye Baby of Queens*

Sonny: *3x American Field Champion, National Amateur Field Champion, Grand Field Champion, Amateur Field Champion, Spanish Corrals Sundance Kid*

GIVING IT TO THE DOGS

I hope you enjoyed this book as much as we enjoy our dogs. If you want to save a dog like Hedlee, there are Brittany rescue organizations that are in dire need of our support. Hedlee came to us through American Brittany Rescue. However, there are two national Brittany rescue organizations that complement each other. One is, of course, American Brittany Rescue. The other is the National Brittany Adoption Network (NBRAN). One dollar will help save a Brittany in need. Please consider donating to:

www.AmericanBrittanyRescue.org

or:

www.nbran.org

How many of you know a dog like Grizzly or Buddy who has died from cancer? I suspect most of you do. The only way to cure cancer for our canine companions is to support organizations that are trying to find a cure, including new treatments and techniques. Every gift matters in the fight against cancer. We need to support cutting edge research, like the work being done by the Morris Animal Foundation.

www.morrisanimalfoundation.org

Acknowledgements

There are a handful of key people who have helped with this book directly or indirectly, many by teaching me about dog psychology, health and care. I first want to thank Dr. Dave and Janice Gantenbein. Janice is Magnolia Hedlee's phenomenal dog trainer. She truly works miracles with dogs. She was Grizzly's trainer for his Eukanuba photo shoot and she continues to help us on issues big and small. Dave has been through every dramatic event with our dogs. He held our puppies when they were days old. He and Janice cared for our newborn puppies when my husband was in the hospital. When the worst day comes and it is time to say goodbye to the dogs we love, it is Dave who is there to hold a paw and to hold our hand. We are honored that Dave and Janice are our dear friends.

I want to thank Nancy Hensley. I was first acquainted with Nancy through events with the American Brittany Club, but our close bond solidified when she became my mentor with American Brittany Rescue after I was chosen to foster Hedlee. Today, Nancy is one of my closest friends. The first day I brought Hedlee home, Nancy called and I told her Hedlee fell asleep in my arms. Hedlee would not willingly let a human touch her until the day I took her home. Who joyfully cried on the phone with me that night? It was Nancy. She has a heart of gold, and she is a triumph in all that is good with American Brittany Rescue.

I want to thank Joy Ory for mentoring me with my teenage dogs, Red and Bear. I have never met someone who is so gentle, patient and kind. She graciously took me under her wing and tried to teach this klutz the art of show. She made my boys look beautiful. Joy is what is right about supporting others in the world of dog shows. I will always call her my friend.

I greatly appreciate and adore Paul and Peggy Doiron, who have field trained Annie, Red, Bear, Moose and Kody. I assure you, Paul and Peggy are the best in the West. I have learned so much from them and I appreciate their kindness over the years. We are fortunate to have had them in our lives and there is no one I trust more with our dogs than this dynamic duo.

From the bottom of my heart, I love all the people who came together to rescue 103-Brittany dogs in Louisiana on that fateful July day. My gratitude goes to rescuer Sue Janowski, who has generously given her time in providing me details of what happened to the dogs once they were seized. She is truly an angel on this earth.

I thank my lucky stars that Janet Fullwood agreed to edit this book. She has a deep love for Brittanys. I admire this strong, beautiful and dynamic woman. She is nothing short of amazing.

Joe Gower, what can I say about you? Thanks for your friendship; because of you (and Sonny) we now have Red and Bear. Our lives have been blessed forever. And no, those pants do not make your butt look big.

There are the people who know me better than anyone else. Thank you to my brother Richard Wollman and his wife, Lori. Your love has uplifted me nearly all my life. Thank you to my Uncle Don and Aunt Marge for giving me important advice and encouragement when it was needed. My deepest gratitude to Larry and Arleene Sommer, who have acted as my surrogate parents for more than two decades. Sometimes, you can choose your family. Lastly, thank you to my husband, Jay, who listened to my laughter and tears as I wrote about us and our Brittany dogs. Without you, we would not have them.

About the Author

If you have read this book, then you really do already know me. I live in a small town in Northern Los Angeles County called Leona Valley. It is pastoral valley with gently rolling terrain bisected by the Amargosa Creek and the San Andreas Earthquake Fault. We chose this place by accident, or perhaps it has chosen us. Either way, we are lucky to call Leona Valley home.

We have seven Brittany dogs. Yes, seven. We love each one for a different reason and are truly blessed to have them in our life. In the last twenty-five years, we have had many Brittanys, but the one that remains deep in our heart is Grizzly, which is why this book is dedicated to his memory.

I wrote about Brittanys being clowns, and it certainly is true. Seven clowns keep us busy while we hold down jobs of our own. I am fortunate to work at home most days, which is why I have witnessed nearly everything these dogs have done. For four of the seven, I was there the moment they took their first breath; and I will be with them the moment they take their last.

They are my family. And now you are, too.

Comments? Email me at Alice@AliceWollman.com

Follow me on Facebook at www.facebook.com/BrittanyDogWriter

95050364R00105

Made in the USA
Lexington, KY
04 August 2018